A sudden vehemence filled her voice. "And yet this spirit cannot have been drained completely away! When you summoned up the energy to go looking, in less than one short day for all your disappointments you found one other person—me—who cares like you! What's one day against the span of history? The world is wide, and we have many days. Let's show that our race still has the audacity to take on an impossible task, and a love for Earth great enough to achieve it!"

Creohan stared at her, hardly able to accept what his ears reported to him. He said blankly, "Do you mean you'd abandon everything on the spur of the moment, commit yourself to a quest that will be likely vain?"

"Why not?" she retorted. "Are you intending to do less? And is it not more worthy of a human being to make a voluntary relinquishment than to have everything snatched away by a grab of blind accident?"

"Yet to turn aside a star!" Creohan whispered, the last writhing of doubt speaking against his will. "I think—I think we must be insane!"

Confidently enough, the girl answered, "Isn't it a glorious madness?"

"THIS IS A QUEST STORY AND A DAMNED GOOD ONE! BRUNNER IS ONE OF THE BETTER SF WRITERS WE HAVE." —*Science Fiction Review*

Also by John Brunner
Published by Ballantine Books:

CATCH A FALLING STAR

JOHN BRUNNER

A Del Rey Book

BALLANTINE BOOKS • NEW YORK

Go and catch a falling star,
  Get with child a mandrake root,
Tell me, where all past years are . . .

JOHN DONNE

I

Desperate for fear the whim that had made the man in gold accept his inspired half-true invitation might evaporate in face of his kind's ineffable contempt for things of today, Creohan silently cursed the doorway of his house for being so slow to open and admit them. There seemed to be a sullen reluctance about the withdrawal of the protective zareba of poisoned thorns, as though the house were growing senile.

Yet perhaps it was only the terror in his mind, bred of his unshared knowledge, that was making seconds feel like hours, minutes like a foretaste of eternity.

The instant the gap was wide enough to admit them, he caught his companion by the arm and hurried him through. Automatically the man in gold resisted; no one could have laid hands on a gold-clad noble of the Lymarian Empire and not felt the chill stroke of just such a jewelled poignard as this counterfeit wore at his waist. But counterfeit he was, all said and done. The resistance was a mere token. Besides, his curiosity had been aroused by Creohan's way of phrasing his invitation.

1

Inwards, then, to the heart of the house, by a moss-floored passage walled with soft-gleaming excrescences shedding an even light, then as they aged deliquescing into a honey-thick substance uttering a delicate fragrance to the air. And, in the midst of the house, the great chamber where the image-field of Creohan's telescope depicted the black sky full of stars.

Too full of stars, by one . . .

Before and after his encounter with the man in gold who alone of all the citizens abroad on the streets tonight had yielded to his importunities, Creohan had been rehearsing in his mind words to bite deep through the armour of indifference. Against this long-hoped-for moment he had planned gestures, declamations, masterly word-pictures to convey the same sense of disaster looming as dominated all his own thoughts. Yet now, coming upon the event in reality rather than imagination, all he could find to say was simply: "Look!"

The man in gold complied, his face showing plainly that he expected more and had no idea what to prepare himself for. A span of time wore away, and he glanced half-angrily back at Creohan.

"This, then, is your device for seeing into the years to come?" he asked. "And this is all that it will show?"

"That star," Creohan said, and pointed. "You never saw it in the sky over your beloved Lymarian Empire, did you?"

"I? How should I know? In that great age men had better things to do o' nights than stare their fill of stars! You cheated me—you lied! You told me you had a way of looking into the future, and I followed you in hopes it might compare with looking at the past. But this— this is nothing!"

Abruptly fury at the smallmindedness of this fellow unlocked Creohan's tongue.

"Is it nothing to know that star will pass so close to Earth that the seas will boil and the land will parch, cities rise in smoke and flame towards the sky—that all the hopes and aspirations of a thousand centuries will be consumed and leave our planet as a barren ball? Is that *nothing?*"

His vehemence took aback the man in gold, who retreated a step, hand falling for reassurance to the hilt of his poignard. "Show me this thing, I say!" he challenged.

Creohan sighed, but he knew already he had failed. "I cannot bring it your sight like the empire whose clothes and manners you affect"—he had almost said: *bad manners.* "But it will surely come about, and in a much lesser space of time in the future than your Lymarians lie into the past."

"How soon?" There was almost greed in the eyes of the man in gold.

"In less than three hundred years."

The man's unease vanished like mist on a sunny morning. He relaxed with a sneer. "Three hundred years? Write it down for your grandchildren to read, then, you fool—by that time I'll be dead, and you, and what shall we know of it? Bah! I should never have believed the promise you made to lure me here."

"I have given you the chance to see into the future," Creohan snapped. "Is it my fault that you lack the wit and will to profit by that chance?"

Very nearly, the sting of the insult caused the man in gold to drag his poignard from its scabbard. But he was no more than a Historicker—a man who spent his life gazing into the dead past with a voyeur's lust—and reason prevailed. They were in Creohan's house, and everyone knew, though few had lived to report, what a house of this kind could do to protect its owner against attack. The Lymarians had had no acquaintance with such homes, but he was not a Lymarian. Clad like one, armed like one, he was still counterfeit.

He spun on his heel, cape swinging out on the air, and strode away muttering curses. Behind him Creohan clutched the supports of the telescope mirror and felt his brain reel under a tidal wave of despair.

Could nothing breach that monstrous wall of human indifference, before the air seared their throats and the hair burned crackling on their heads?

Across the object mirror of the telescope the image of the stellar runaway crawled. As yet it was tiny. He might never have paid it any special attention, but for Molichant.

That small, dark, astute man was a Historicker likewise, but of a kind Creohan found bearable: not an addict consumed by jealousy for some long-distant day when, as he deluded himself, he could have found outlets in real life for some quality of heroism or some fancied skill, but one concerned to know how things became as they were, conducting a rational quest among the mazes of the past for the cause of this, or that, or the other contemporary phenomenon.

Perhaps because the majority of his fellows were indeed addicts, over the past year or two he had taken to calling on Creohan occasionally to discuss what he had learned. To talk of his discoveries with other Historickers would, in Creohan's cynical view, have been fruitless; argument would rapidly have degenerated into vain screaming, and perhaps even fighting, over the comparative virtues of a dozen great periods of history.

In return, Molichant suffered Creohan's talk about the stars with good grace, and even sometimes furnished him with useful information about the changing patterns of the sky as they appeared over the accessible range of millennia. And, lately, he had happened to mention that this star now so bright had not been visible in the time of the Mending of Men, a scant ten centuries before.

Intrigued, Creohan had indulged in a few measurements, a little calculation—the sort of thing he loved. He had catalogued the local proper motions long before, and disregarded this particular star as having nothing remarkable to attract his attention. And an increase in brightness over the decade or so of his studies was too marginal to be significant; there were many stars whose radiation fluctuated by the odd per cent either way.

A thousand years, though, gave an adequate baseline for computation. And last night, out of idle curiosity, he had made use of it.

Until dawn he had sat checking and re-checking the figures, eliminating every possibility of error; drugged himself at last to sleep in the faint, faint hope that today he would prove himself wrong; woken again and gone back, foodless, haggard, to repeat the entire series of equations. There was no mistake. In two hundred and eighty-eight years that star would cross the limits of the solar system. It would be drawn inwards to circle the sun in a dwindling spiral until the two united in a giant hell of flames.

Only there would be no one to see it—on Earth.

Confronted, alone, with that intolerable burden of knowledge, Creohan had wished fervently he could have been born a Historicker by inclination, or a Druggist, or a Coupler—anything that would have saved him from having to meddle with the knowledge of reality. Perhaps he had gone briefly mad, for there was a gap in his memory; from his table at home he seemed to have passed directly to the streets of the city, without decision to move.

All afternoon and evening he had walked the streets, accosting strangers, being rebuffed or laughed away. The man in gold had been his last hope. A flash of inspiration had supplied the promise of a glimpse into the future, and the man—a sensation-seeker above all—had taken the bait.

To no purpose.

Creohan clenched his fists in impotent rage. Did these people feel no gratitude to Earth, which had brought forth the manifold richness they turned to their unworthy ends? Was their power of vision wholly limited to the span of their selfish little lives? Had they lost all love for the planet which bore them? If he brought himself to believe that, he could not endure to go on living! It would not seem worth being a member of the human race.

Surely, somewhere, if not in this city then in another, he must find a companion who would weep with him for a disaster which would not occur in his own lifetime. There were, after all, so many people, and of so many different kinds.

His tumultuous mind calmed a little. Given a link to the quiet, reasonable days of the vanished past (was it only yesterday when the past ended? It seemed like an eon ago!), he was able to order his thoughts. He had hit on a subject he had frequently discussed with Molichant, in ordinary conversational style. He commanded the house to conjure up the man's likeness in the air, and—having gathered an excellent impression of him on his repeated visits—the house complied so effectively that Creohan all but addressed his friend aloud.

If only he could have been here in person . . .

But at their last meeting Molichant had expressed his intention of trailing some triviality—the form of a current word, maybe, or a snatch of melody: Creohan had forgotten what—into the very deep past indeed, and from a trip of that order he would not return in less than twenty days.

And if he were physically present, I think I might—

Shocked and horrified, Creohan chopped the thought off in the instant of its conception. To revenge himself on a friend for facts which were the fault of the universe—no, that was a shameful impulse, such as he was dismayed to find in himself. It could not be better to linger in blissful ignorance, though he might wistfully envy the fortune of those who had no inkling of the doom awaiting this planet. Molichant had done him a service by guiding him to his discovery, and indeed, provided all spirit had not been leached out of the people of this modern age, might have done a service for the whole of mankind.

Concentrating on that argument, Creohan composed himself with his eyes fixed on the image of his friend and reviewed the common course of the many chats they had had on what for the moment seemed an all-important theme.

II

"HAVE YOU NOT thought"—so Creohan would customarily say—"that in another few centuries men like yourself will be yearning back towards this day and age, our own, and finding it superior to theirs? Yet you, and all those who share your passion for Historicism, turn aside from it, neglect it, think it beneath your notice! I'll wager you know more of the way the world wagged in the time of the Mending of Men than of what is going on abroad this very instant."

He had thought Molichant, specializing in a period less than ten centuries ago—moderation as Historicism went—would be vulnerable to such an argument. But it seemed to slide past him, and he accorded it no more than a chuckle, the kind with which one acknowledges a casual witticism.

"Find this bland age superior? Why, compared to theirs, maybe it will appear so! Maybe each age is indeed inferior to its predecessors."

Then, noticing the stony look on Creohan's face which disdained joking, he would hunch forward, both hands clasped around a mug of that particular wine

offered by his host's home which he preferred, it not
being secreted by his own house, and shift to a margi-
nally more serious tone.

"Oh, there is much evidence one can advance for
such a view! It has been established, for example, that
these houses which so cosset and protect us are not a
product of the natural order of life, but cunningly fash-
ioned by subtle tampering with vegetable heredity;
where today can you find me such an artificer as he
who contrived the first of them? Likewise the lights that
hover nightly in the sky, and render us independent of
the fixed return of the sun—there was an age, not
overlong since, when the air was empty of them and
men had perforce to stumble around bearing torches if
they wished to venture abroad after sundown. All this
you must grant me, must you not?"

"I cede it willingly," was Creohan's reply. "For it
digs a deep pitfall across the pathway of your logic.
Consider! You choose a time to expend your attention
on which, by the clock of the universe, lies a mere
eyeblink into the past. Another who goes with you to
the Houses of History will sneer at the time of the
Mending of Men, and linger only when he encounters
the Brydwal, claiming that their exploitation of the
senses of the human body represented the pinnacle of
all our millennia of achievement; a second will envy the
abdication of personal responsibility achieved by the
Gerynts, and mock the excessive concern the Brydwal
exhibited with the subjective responses of the indi-
vidual; still a third will class both these as extremist,
and maintain that the Minogovaristo were ideal, as
having hit upon the balanced compromise. Is it not so?"

And, on Molichant's cautious nod of agreement, he
uttered in triumph his insoluble paradox. "On your
argument that each age declines from its predecessors,

why does not every Historicker go back as far as possible?"

Molichant shrugged. "In the last resort it's something unsusceptible of definition which lures a man to the Houses of History. Had you even a spark of what we feel by instinct, as it were, I'd not need to sit here and argue over it. You might, however, say that some people, owing to their ancestry and their way of thinking, feel better suited to ages other than their own. The infinite variety of cultures and societies which our imagination has brought about must hold something for everyone by now."

"No, that cannot be so. Otherwise how account for such as I, who feel no least attraction from what I'm told of any bygone age?"

"Perhaps I was exaggerating," Molichant admitted after a pause. "An alternative occurs to me: that the lure may lie in the security one feels when experiencing an age of which one knows the outcome."

"Is there, then, so much insecurity in this modern age?" Creohan countered. "From what can it stem? Anciently it derived from the fear of hunger, or the threat of storm and winter-cold. Who today risks starvation, who is stricken by poverty? Why, even the ultimate shadow of death is lessened by the knowledge that through the Houses of History another may endlessly re-witness one's most petty doings!"

"Why, then, look on it as an antidote to boredom," Molichant said in a cross tone. "Apparently nothing closer to the truth will penetrate the armour of your preconceptions!"

At which point the dispute would hang fire, unresolved. Creohan had often suspected that at bottom Molichant was still smarting from his original failure to persuade his friend that he ought to sample, at least, the experiences which for him were the entire reason for living, and he had no wish to re-open a stale argument for fear of spoiling the liking that had grown up between them on other grounds.

Coming back from memory, he dismissed the image of the Historicker, and as it faded thought again of one justification he had advanced for his pursuits. Now the outcome of this age that he and Molichant and everyone else lived in was known: did that make it more acceptable? Would Molichant become more secure, sharing Creohan's knowledge? Of course not! He and all his kind would flee further and more often into years gone by.

He desired to see the sky direct, instead of through the intermediacy of the telescope, and the roof of the chamber folded back like a tired flower, leaving him standing in the open. There was something he had never questioned, and now he started to wonder about the workings of it, as though in the moment when he realized it must end, Earth had become a source of total and complete fascination for him.

The house had been—not a part of him, exactly, but—an extension of him, since he acquired it. He had selected it because of its telescope; before he came along it had stood empty, as all houses had to, forgetting its previous owner. Perhaps he had been a little too hasty to move in. Even now it occasionally displayed a trait he did not recognise as his own, and conversely he wondered now and then whether some of the habits he did so recognise might not have been unconsciously inherited from his predecessor.

Once, a few years ago, he had been sufficiently moved by curiosity to ask the house, "Who was your former occupier? Can you show him to me?"

The room shivered; the whole house seemed to strain in recollection. But by that time it did in fact know only Creohan as owner, and the image it projected for him was a slightly younger version of himself.

Well, it didn't matter. The one-time owner of this house would—seeing that he had centered his home around this telescope—presumably have understood the emotions which now racked Creohan. But he must be long dead. There was only one way to find out who he had been, short of frustrating and probably pointless inquiries of all the citizens, and that was to turn Historicker. He had considered asking Molichant to investigate for him, but decided against it. The answer would almost certainly have been that here was the ideal opportunity to sample for himself the wonders of a House of History.

Cool night breezes tugged at his full beard as he stood listening to the clamour and fitful music of the city going about its nighttime affairs. In the far distances he could faintly discern the insane laughter of the next day's meat as it assembled on the gentle slopes of the hills inland prior to descending to the shore and there making rendezvous with its predestined master, Death. Overhead hordes of circling lights blinded the populace against the stars.

On impulse he whistled one of the lights down to him, recalled belatedly that it could not come until he had ordered a cessation of the soft vibrations which his house emitted from tympanic membranes to clear the field of vision for the telescope; set that to rights, and whistled once again. The light complied, and he gazed at it as it perched on his outstretched hand, its mindless head cocked on one side, its beady eyes closed. This one was green, for his street was green and had been for the past week—roadway, the walls of the houses, and in consequence the lights circling in the air. Some elementary reflex drew them always to places of their own colour.

Although Molichant had specifically cited the existence of the lights as the continuing proof that some past age had enjoyed skills that now were lost, he had never given the creatures much thought. They appeared nightly, served their purpose, and went away, a simple fact of modern living. Now he found himself wondering about them with a kind of hunger. Did they eat? They must, but if so, what? Surely, too, they must breed and reproduce. Where? Would it serve any purpose to inquire among Historickers about their origins, suffering the inevitable boastfulness each displayed about his preferred segment of the past until he learned when and in what manner they were brought about?

No, probably not. He sighed. Historickers like Molichant were rare. The majority preferred to contemplate uncritically the vanished wonders of another age, and lacked the persistence to make complex inquiries into their mode of operation.

He shook the creature back into the sky, and it spread its radiance-shedding wings and resumed its aimless circling among its fellows.

From the hills the breeze again brought the half-ecstatic, half-agonised screams of the meat, and his mind was once more darting off at a tangent. That was something Molichant could justly have invoked along with lights and houses to prop his thin argument about modern decadence: the daily arrival of sufficient meat, its willingness to greet Death as a friend and serve the people of this city. Doubtless the idea had escaped him because, like Creohan, he seldom partook of meat except when dining with a friend. He and Creohan both were exceptionally fortunate in their homes, that were still versatile enough to furnish all their dietary needs; there was no question of principle involved.

And many people, Creohan glossed greyly, still clung to the superstitious notion that some extra, indescribably subtle contagion would convey vigour from food which had itself been vigorous a few hours earlier into their own bodies.

Are we all grown foolish in our decline? The question loomed unbidden at the fringe of Creohan's awareness. *Are we as a species bordering on senility, so that the doom of the approaching star will offer merciful euthanasia?*

"No!" he cried aloud, and the sound startled a few of the hovering lights, so that they flapped wildly and withdrew to higher levels.

No, the suggestion was intolerable. To accept it would be to accept that argument of Molichant's to which he had given the lie, and concede that there was something in past history for every person now alive; hence, the human race had exhausted its powers of invention.

Once more, he decided, *once* more, he would make the attempt to find a companion to lament the fate of Earth. He could hope for no more than a fellow-mourner's solace—he had no means to turn a star aside from its course. But regret was the very least that Man could offer to his mother-world.

Somewhere in the city, then, he must find the person he sought. Or if not in the city, then out in the wide world—inland across the plains of Cruin, or beyond the near and far Arbelline Oceans . . .

Somewhere. *Somewhere!*

He needed a means to impress on people the seriousness of his pleading. After a moment's thought, he commanded the house to give him a suit of mourning clothes: a hat with a brim that cast a melancholy shadow on his face, a slashed tunic the colour of drying blood, and leggings that appeared to be plastered from ankle to knee with slowly crusting mud.

Arrayed in this garb, Creohan set out to find his fellow-mourner.

III

For hours he walked, up this street and down that, until he was growing giddy with fatigue, hunger and despair. And, moreover, with the monotony of variety that the city afforded to his eyes. No two houses anywhere were alike, because no two people were alike, and where a couple, a group or family of more than one generation shared a single dwelling the complexity of interaction between them rendered their home fantastical. Sheer randomness made it impossible to deduce by abstract principle where any given house was located; the names, even, which each street bore were outworn traditional terms. His own was called "Of the Musicians", but to his knowledge no musician had lived there in a decade or more.

Currently it was, indeed, superficially united into a whole, by the shared green tint which stretched from end to end and dictated the colour of the hovering lights above it. But that too was a fickle phenomenon, brought about by the chance cycle of the sluggish metabolisms of the houses and their habit of adopting reflexively the tint of whichever was for the moment most vigorous. Last week the Street of the Musicians had been blue, and before that orange-yellow, and the Street of the Travellers beyond it was white.

Ordinarily that would have been of interest to Creohan. Often, when he wanted a white light for some special task and the natural luminance of his house's walls was inadequate, he needed to go and whistle one down, hood it and carry it home. Now, though, he could not conceive of himself wishing to attack any other task than the one of finding his fellow-mourner.

Apart from Historickers—and at this time of night most of them were mentally far away in the past— people generally affected clothing of the same colour as their street was currently, as though they could not be sure who their neighbours and friends were without outward evidence of conformity. The folk walking abroad waved to others similarly clad, embraced and exchanged warm words of greeting. To one wearing mourning clothes, however, none chose to speak, and on Creohan's addressing them the people he stopped returned a blank, uncomfortable gaze and no attention.

Before a house on a street whose name he did not know, over the door of which hung a sign announcing that the inhabitants were poets and calligraphers and would furnish for a small fee unparalleled verses on any subject in the Yandish, Fragial or Cleophine scripts, he encountered a youth attired in tufts of hair at elbows, knees and ankles much occupied in nibbling at the plump pale shoulders of a woman older than himself. In a voice harsh with desperation Creohan demanded what it would cost to have made a powerful and affecting ballad on the end of the world.

The youth ceased his attentions to the woman for an instant of reflection. "It's a stale subject," he announced at last. "The minstrel Scrand exhausted it five thousand years ago. And who any longer derives enjoyment from the work of Scrand?"

The woman favoured Creohan with a scowl, and guided the poet's writhing lips to the lobe of her left ear.

In an open space where recently a house had died, and as yet the ground was too impoverished for new seeds to take root, a girl was forming shapes of coloured smoke, watched by three awed children below the age of puberty. To her likewise Creohan spoke, demanding if she could make a great display visible throughout the city, of sombre roiling fumes lit with such flame as might depict the incineration of a planet. She paid no heed; when finally he touched her arm uncertainly, she raised her face to give him a sweet smile and drew back curtains of dark hair either side of her head to touch her ears and signify that she was deaf.

Shuddering a little, he passed on, and came at last with purpose unaccomplished to the edge of the sea. There a broad road curved with the shore around a bay, on towards a headland where it vanished from sight. A quiet succession of waves rolled beachward from the ocean, leaving the land's fringe of sand littered with crabs and molluscs dying in luminescent pulses of ice-green and white. In response a few white and green lights circled overhead, but the road was sombre purple like a shadow, and the lights directly above him were so few they did not altogether blot out the stars.

Despondent, he sought among them for the runaway which boded mankind's doom, and saw it slanting towards the horizon, for the night was far advanced. He stared at it long and long, half-minded to abandon his quest already. For who, lacking the insight years of work with his telescope had given him, would credit danger arising from something so innocent and beautiful as a sparkling light on the backdrop of space?

At length he roused himself and looked around. Not far off, a solitary tavern grew from the beach. He had not been into one for years; taverns were patronised mainly by folk whose own homes were inadequate, through youth or age. Now, though, his nerves were jangling, and liquor would be welcome. Besides, someone lounging in a tavern would be less likely to move away before he could speak his knowledge than someone stopped at random on the street.

He made towards it. Like all taverns, it was circular. Seven rooms disposed like a chambered snail-shell spiralled outwards from a central hall, and in this centre was the waiter, blind, slow-thinking, and at anyone's service to grant any refreshment within its power.

That dull green knob, high as a man and studded with the sphinctered projections from which it served the clients, did not ask what he wanted as he entered. It was content to wait, immobile as the jugs on the low counter ringing it, placid as the sea outside.

Voices and laughter could be heard from some of the curved side-rooms, but the customers there were out of sight. In the central room at the moment Creohan walked in there was only one other person, a gross woman in dark clothing, staring at the ceiling with blank unfocused eyes. At first he paid her no attention, mentally debating which of the available infinity of liquors he should select, but while he was still pondering she moved, leaning over the low counter and applying her lips directly to a projection on the waiter, like an infant at the breast.

Instantly there was a tingling all down Creohan's spine. He spun, and gave the woman an astonished glance. The drab black chiton which was her sole garment, the attitude she had adopted as she sucked, made all clear in an instant. She was a Historicker addicted to the period of the Glorious Gerynts, and what she was imbibing could only be . . .

Horrorstruck, he saw how her heavy body sagged and heaved with her gulping and made her chiton stretch and hang loose by turns. That was the Gerynt way; they had scorned ornament and decoration. And when one of their contemporary imitators reached this phase, the best place to be was somewhere else.

He made for the door, walking cat-soft, but before he could reach it she had ceased her sucking, turned bleary eyes on him, and shot out a fat arm with dismaying speed to block his way. Helpless, not a little frightened, he stopped dead.

"You mourn?" she said thickly, when she had completed her survey of his appearance. "It is not the custom to mourn in a tavern. It is unfitting!"

The leaden delivery of the words confirmed Creohan's worst fears. Intrigued sufficiently at long last, she had come here to try the Gerynts' "blood of women" for herself. The waiter, as was its function, had provided what she asked for, and now the co-life would be whispering its sibilant words inside her brain. Thrice a year the Gerynts had imbibed their drink from the full breasts of their lobotomised repositories of right thinking, for in their day the co-life could only be kept alive in a human environment. Once in a lifetime was too often for a citizen of the modern age.

"Give me poison," Creohan said to the waiter. "In a jug."

He hated himself for what he was about to do, but regret was fruitless. As when he had found himself impelled to hate Molichant for bringing the terrible news to him, he was laying blame at the wrong door. If anyone should be blamed, it must be the Gerynts themselves, and they were far out of reach behind the veil of time.

Ice-cold liquor that burned with a black glow rushed from a living spigot. Before the jug was a quarter full the woman spoke again.

"Whom do you mourn, or is your mourning a lie?"

"I mourn for Earth," Creohan said, one eye on the rising level in the jug, and knew as he uttered the words that he had made a mistake. The co-life that had entered the woman's brain was remorseless—that was why the Gerynts had disappeared.

"Earth is not alive and therefore cannot be dead," the woman stated. "Earth is still in existence, and therefore it is false to claim to mourn it. You are plainly either incapable of logical reasoning, or very dishonest. In either case it is a public duty to dispose of you!"

Just so had the Gerynts thought and spoken; for that reason too they had disappeared.

Grunting, the woman heaved herself to her feet and caught hold of an empty jug on the counter, intending to use it as a club on Creohan's head. At the same moment the jug of poison was filled; he snatched at it and dashed it in his attacker's face. The liquid splashed widely. One drop landed on his own hand, and the thumb tingled and went numb. But the woman, with a moan of vague astonishment, keeled over and lay still.

She was finished, but the co-life that shared her brain was not; seeking escape, it oozed from the openings of her ears. Hastily Creohan wiped his hand and poured the last few dregs of poison onto the thing's naked protoplasm, drawing what small consolation he could from this visible proof of the rightness of his action. It writhed and died.

Stunned, dismayed, horrified, he fumbled the jug back to the counter. The waiter said suddenly, "You asked for poison."

He nodded, forgetting it could not see, and it went on, "You are not dead. When one orders poison, one ought to die. Was it not strong poison?"

"It was very strong poison," said Creohan, forcing the words past a filthy taste overspreading his tongue. "Is it not enough that one should be dead? The poison did not go to waste."

With that he stumbled blindly forward, so dazed that he mistook the direct exit to the clean ocean air and went instead through the spiralling private rooms. The first was occupied, but the clients there were Couplers, intent on establishing in how many ways their bodies might be conjoined, and far too preoccupied to notice any intrusion. Leaving them, he came to another occupied room, where sat three women and a man watching a creature picked up on the seashore die in a series of graceful gyrations. The last of its antics coincided with Creohan's entrance, and, reaching to reclaim their tall mugs of bluish liquor, they looked up and saw him.

"Whom do you mourn?" said one of the women merrily. "This thing here?" She impaled the fresh corpse with the sharp nail on one index finger and held it up to show him.

"I lament that the world will soon end," Creohan said mechanically.

"That will save us having to think of new ways to pass the time," said the same woman; her male companion, more practically, muttered, "The man's deranged."

"How is this thing to happen?" demanded a second woman, part of whose face was hidden under a samite mask.

"Another sun is going to burn Earth up."

"Another sun? There isn't but one sun," said the first woman. "Unless we get a new sun every day—I never thought of that."

"There are thousands of suns!" snapped Creohan. "All the stars are suns!"

"Stars?" echoed the woman uncomprehendingly. The masked woman spoke up.

"The litttle lights in the sky! You've seen them."

"I've seen them, yes, but I never heard them called by any such name," said the first woman. "Besides, they aren't anything like hot enough to burn up the world. They're barely even warm. And they flutter—like this!" She waved her arms in imitation of the night-flying lights, and gave the man of the party cause to regret having chosen that moment to raise his drink to his lips. During the recriminations that followed, Creohan fled, sick half with nausea at what he had had to do to the woman in the black chiton, half with pure shame at what had become of the race spawned by his beloved Earth.

IV

Why am I running?

The question rattled around Creohan's skull like a pea jumping in a hollow drum: rational, but not enough to halt the pounding of his feet on the wet beach-sand. There could be no hurry now in any task he might undertake. Even the quest for a fellow-mourner could, if he chose, occupy the rest of his life. It was not, after all, as though there were something he could do to avert the fate of Earth.

And yet he could not escape from an overwhelming sense of urgency, as if every day he spent on this doomed planet would now be wasted unless it held some meaningful action directed towards . . .

Towards what? Turning aside a gigantic ball of flaming gas called a star? It was ridiculous!

So it was not the call of reason that put an end to his mad flight along the beach, but only the upheaval of his belly, that ultimately revolted at the memory of the black-clad woman's death and doubled him over as surely as a blow to the pit of his stomach, convulsing him like a live frog spitted on a hot iron.

One hand supporting him against a nearby rock, he gasped and retched and spat and almost wept until the necessary foulness of his deed was purged from him. Then, weakened, he remained for a while with head bowed, assuring himself again of the harsh truth that had he not done as he did the woman who sought to ape the Glorious Gerynts would herself have consigned him and possibly many others to oblivion for no better reason than that the co-life in her brain disapproved of their clothing or the way they dressed their hair.

Eventually a curious fact intruded on his awareness: the rock on which his hand was resting did not feel like rock, but like rough cloth. Confused, he was trying to comprehend that when a voice spoke sweetly out of nowhere: the voice of a girl.

"You're sick, friend! Is there something I can do to help?"

He raised his eyes. Here, the rocks that studded the shore broached the limit of the water. A few paces seaward of him, up to her knees, long dark hair sparkling as it shed droplets which caught the random flash of the circling lights above, the speaker stood gazing at him. How long she had been there he could not tell.

Effortlessly he formed words with his much-abused mouth. "I thank you—no. It was only something which . . . But never mind. It's gone to the past and cannot be amended."

Relieved, the girl came forward and, with a murmur of excuse, eased from beneath his numb hand the rough cloth that his skin had paradoxically reported—a towel to dry herself. She was quite unclad and not at all abashed about it. Why should she be? Her body, Creohan noted as he regained command of his normal self, was slender and exquisitely formed; at the moment the towel wrapped around and hid her, a dying light wheeled by and cast a momentary glow before it fell into the sea, enough to show him that her face too was beautiful, broad and underlain by strong bones.

Yet her appearance, seemingly from the ocean itself, was a mystery to him. Fumbling, he shaped awkward words.

"Did you—did you come out of the sea?"

"Of course! Why not?" the girl said, and gave a trilling laugh as she gathered handfuls of her dark tresses and wrung water from them, drip-drip-drip. "I've been out there seeing what there is to see. I do it nightly, and often in the day as well."

"*Under* the water? Surely it's not possible to breathe down there!"

"I doubt if my friends down there would be so cruel as to let me drown," the girl said with a shrug. The motion exposed her breast above the towel, and she glanced down as though approving its form before wiping off the last trace of water.

This was all new and strange to Creohan. He said slowly, "There are people in the sea, then?"

"People? You might call them people, I suppose," the girl replied. She deftly twisted her towel into a sort of snood around her wet hair and reached for a garment likewise draped upon the rock, which she drew on against the nighttime cool. "And not only people— things! Oh, they're so beautiful!"

She checked almost before the last words were uttered. "Do you truly not know what can be found beneath the waves?" she demanded. "A shame, a shame! If I'd not tired myself out with overmuch swimming tonight, I'd take you now and show you what there is, for it's so—so *beautiful!*"

"There too?" said Creohan, half to himself. "Why, that's all the greater pity that the world should end."

The girl, engaged in rubbing at her hair, caught the faint words and stared at him. "End?" she repeated uncertainly. "Why should it end? It has gone on for thousands of years, so I believe—not so?"

Creohan did not answer her directly. He said instead, "Would you join with me in regretting its passing?"

"Of course I would! But I don't understand what you mean." The girl fixed him with her large dark eyes, seeming deep as the ocean whose praises she had sung.

He extended his arm, pointing. "Do you see that star?"

She turned to follow the direction he indicated, and said, "Ah—the greenish one?"

"No, the bluish, very bright and almost at the horizon."

She hesitated. After a moment, she stepped close to him and put her cheek against his upper arm so that she might the better follow his pointing finger. "Yes, I see it," she said. "What of it?"

"That is a sun about as large as ours. In a short while—longer than our lifetimes, but shorter than the times Historickers go back to—it will come so close that it will burn the Earth to ashes."

"A sun? Like the one which shines on us by day?"

"They are all suns. Perhaps they have worlds like ours circling them—who knows?"

The girl shivered; Creohan felt the movement through the light contact of her head against his arm. She said, "To think I have lived all my life without wondering about the nature of the sky . . . It must be a great place up there, greater by far than my little world beneath the sea. Tell me about it!"

She reached back, unlooking, with both hands to find a level section of the edge of the rock, and sprang

backwards up to it. With bare legs swinging she sat
there and attended to Creohan as he spoke softly of the
knowledge he had had from his telescope, and from the
ancient work of many, many vanished scientists: about
the great empty deeps between those spangled lights,
the stars; about the heat and fury which, close to, the
innocent jewels of the sky poured forth; about the
fabled voyages that could be traced only in half-missing
legends, supposedly preceding the furthest explorations
of Historickers, beyond the comforting armour of
Earth's atmosphere . . .

In her turn, too, she spoke, and told of the friends
she had made beneath the sea, not people exactly, but
creatures of whom some were quite intelligent and all
were curious, so that when a visitor swam down among
the hollow coral grottoes they inhabited they would
emerge, chanting a sort of booming song of welcome
that made the ears complain and the very skin tingle,
and bringing with them certain kinds of gas-filled water-
weed, which nipped between the teeth furnished the
means of breathing—after some practice—so that one
might go for hours through their jewelled underwater
caverns, alight with singing mobile creatures that
glowed red and white and yellow and green.

And they spoke of many other things besides, including matters that Creohan had never before discussed with anybody. They talked of the threatening
star below the horizon, and others along with it, until
the gaudy colours of dawn began to tint the sky.

Only then did Creohan remember to stretch his
cramped body and yawn, which last turned into a short
bitter laugh. "Thank you for hearing me out," he said.
"All day and the earlier part of tonight I have been
hunting for someone who would merely listen to me.
But no one seems to care!"

"No one?" said the girl quietly. "*I* care."

"You do indeed, and that's a miracle. But . . . Well, for me it was as though the truth I'd learned had transformed the world. On the instant it was no longer the same place as yesterday. And—it is, and also it isn't." His fingers curled òver to his palms, as though trying to shape forms of air which would convey his precise meaning. "Those people I met in the tavern, whom I told you of: *they* don't care because they don't know how to care! Some bored, so that one of them could say that the end of the world would save her and her friends from having to think of new ways to pass their time—some obsessed by repeating erotic acts that cannot possibly be novel because our bodily form has not changed in more time than Historickers can estimate— and as for the woman whom I had to kill . . ."

He bowed his head, words failing him. Equally silent, the girl laid a comforting arm around his shoulders and waited until he could speak again. Lightly he brushed her fingers with his own, to signal thanks, and resumed.

"And yet even people like her, in some sense, have an important gift: the power to commit themselves wholly to a cause in which they believe. Is not the ending of our world a cause to demand the attention of everyone? I'd scarcely have imagined that it could not be. Yet I've found proof by actual trial. Most of our race would rather live and laugh and love, and there's an end of it. They know that they'll be dead before this disaster happens, so they pay it no heed. It seems to me as though my friend Molichant is right: the spirit that motivated the lusty ages Historickers retire to has been drained from our modern breed!"

"I could believe that." The girl nodded. "Since I

ceased to be a child I've spent much time alone, because so few of the people I've met are like myself. What word should I use? I'd say 'curious', I suppose—as, being curious, I went to see what was in the ocean for the very first time. And yet—"

A sudden vehemence filled her voice. "And yet this spirit cannot have been drained completely away! When you summoned up the energy to go looking, in less than one short day for all your disappointments you found one other person—me—who cares like you! What's one day against the span of history? The world is wide, and we have many days. Let's show that our race still has the audacity to take on an impossible task, and a love for Earth great enough to achieve it! So there is no one but us here who loves adventure, welcomes challenges, dares to try and dictate the shape of tomorrow—why should such a person stay here, among a gang of self-indulgent lazybones? With all the world before us, why should we?"

Creohan stared at her, hardly able to accept what his ears reported to him. He said blankly, "Do you mean you'd abandon everything on the spur of the moment, commit yourself to a quest that will be likely vain?"

"Why not?" she retorted. "Are you intending to do less? And is it not more worthy of a human being to make a voluntary relinquishment than to have everything snatched away by a grab of blind accident?"

"Oh, yes!" Creohan said in a low voice. "Yes, yes, *yes!*"

He caught her hand and drew her to her feet. Standing together they lifted their eyes towards the sky where it was paling from black into blue with the coming of sunrise.

"Yet to turn aside a star!" Creohan whispered, the

last writhing of doubt speaking against his will. "I think—I think we must be insane!"

Confidently enough, the girl answered, "Isn't it a glorious madness?"

Nonetheless, he felt that the hand she had linked with his was very cold, and she was trembling.

V

THEY FINALLY WEARIED of their staring and made to depart, and in the same instant a point struck Creohan to which he gave immediate voice.

"Why!" he exclaimed. "We have talked all these hours and I still do not know your name or place of residence. I am called Creohan, and I live on the Street of the Musicians."

"My name is Chalyth," the girl responded. "And as for my home—why, here or anywhere, all about and around."

"You have taken no house of your own?"

"What need has one of a house? I have few belongings. The nights are always warm, and when rain falls there are trees and shrubs to shelter under. But I love the touch of water on my skin, so I seldom hide from the wetness of mere rain."

"But—but food!" Creohan fumbled. "And clothing!"

"Are those not always to be had? For all their faults the people of our city are generous—as why should they not be when what they give away costs them nothing? This shift grows thin." She plucked up the hem of it. "Tomorrow or the next day or whenever it wore out, I'd need to do no more than look out for another girl my size and put my request to her; likewise for food, or else the people of the sea would give me something strange and good to bring back to the air with me and savour on the beach, still tingling with the sharp salt of the ocean. We have a rich and bountiful world, and there's enough for all."

This was so far from Creohan's own rootedness, his attachment to his home with its beloved telescope and the zareba of thorns before the entrance, that he shook his head in wonder, and she laughed openly at his bewilderment.

"Tell me truly!" she cried. "Could someone anchored by possessions suggest so lightly that we depart on our quest?"

He hesitated, then admitted, "No. Indeed I myself feel put to shame by your words. But for the lucky chance of meeting you I could envisage myself in fifty years from now, a gnarled and bitter old man, still clutching at the sleeves of passers-by, still in this same city which I'd then have sifted over and over without finding anyone to heed my warning, until at last the people would shun me, thinking me deranged. Should we start out now before my courage dies? If so, which way?" He looked about the land now lit by the beginning of day, and saw that the dull purple lights which had hovered above the road were climbing high and fading out of sight.

Once more Chalyth laughed. "Oh, hardly, Creohan! To go about the world at random as you about the city would be to mock at good fortune. Where one searcher must guess, two may discuss and make a proper plan. Besides, there are preparations, and chief among these"—she fought, and failed to master, a yawn—"would be some rest."

"Come with me, then," Creohan said.

"Yes, I will. Whatever I think of tying oneself to a house, I can foresee that on our journey it may be long and long before we lie in one again."

So they went companionably back into the city and in Creohan's house lay down together on his broad soft couch, green and springy as good turf and always kept to human temperature. There they embraced without passion but with a kind of matter-of-fact friendliness that filled his mind with confidence to quiet his former terror, and drifted with limbs entwined into sleep as untroubled as a happy child's.

Noon past, they rose, and from the resources of the house clad themselves already in garments fit for a long difficult journey, flame-red shirts and loose grey breeches, and soft tough boots resistant to a stony road. They broke their fast in the chamber of the telescope, almost without talking, until suddenly Creohan raised his voice and commanded the house to rid the room of its dominant feature.

At once their ears were filled with a complaining sound, but he was obeyed. The great mirror dulled; the strong supports withered and cracked like old dry branches before a forest fire; the house re-absorbed his treasure into its substance, and the chamber seemed as empty as the deeps of space.

"Why did you that?" Chalyth cried. "Was it not what you chiefly prized?"

"Once it was," Creohan said grimly. "But I remembered what you said last night—that no one encumbered with possessions would lightly propose setting forth on the road we must take. What use would my telescope be to me now? All it could do would be to tempt me to stare at that disastrous star, and eat out my heart with sorrow. If I need confirmation of our purpose, I need only gaze upwards; it's bright enough now to signal danger to my mind without artificial aids."

Across the table at which they sat Chalyth looked at him, and her eyes brimmed with tears.

"It's done," he said gruffly. "And done for a purpose, what is more. I take it as a good omen. So! Which way shall we go?"

Chalyth swallowed hard, and blinked away her tears, and countered with a question of her own in an equally level voice. "In the city there's a street they call the Street of Travellers. Is there anyone dwelling there who has indeed explored the land around?"

Creohan grimaced. "Hah! Whenever it was that they gave our streets their names, it must have been long ago; there are, likely as many travellers on the street called after them as there are musicians here on mine, which is none at all. So— Wait, though!" His face brightened. "Now that I think of it, there is indeed one man who justifies that name, and lives there, too. I heard of him from Molichant, who said that he's now old, but that in his youth he voyaged out across the ocean and found strange marvellous things."

"How is he called?"

"Glyre, if I remember right."

"Then there's where we begin our search," said Chalyth.

But when they came to Glyre's home there was no answer to their calls, and as they shouted a neighbour of his spoke up, to convey distressing news.

"It's no use you shouting after *him*," he said—a lean man growing old, resting on a swing of red-leaved creepers. "If he's at home he likely will not answer, being much distracted. That's the trouble with these Historickers."

"He's turned Historicker?" said Creohan, dismayed.

"Why, certainly! Do you not know this tale he's so fond of repeating to everyone, how in his youth he voyaged out to sea and found an ancient city, its towers crumpled by the fist of time? These many years past he's been determined to view it in its prime, and I suppose has managed to."

"I think I know that city," said Chalyth. "One of my friends beneath the sea brought me a golden helmet as a gift, which was too large for me and I declined it. He said in the way such creatures have that he had swum many times faster than a boat can travel for a day and a night to reach the shore on which such things are littered by the thousand. It was not known to him how long ago the city fell."

"If Glyre is not at home," Creohan asked the man in the swing, "where would he likely be—at the House of History?"

The man shrugged. "Oh, probably. But which among them all, I couldn't say. The present is enough for me. To past and future alike I feel indifferent."

From the twined strands of creeper supporting him he drew down evidence of the reason for his attitude: the mouthpiece of a long tube filled with subtle narcotics. Placing it to his lips, he inhaled deeply, and on the instant forgot about Creohan, Chalyth and his neighbour Glyre.

"Ach!" Chalyth whispered. "I do not like Druggists!"

"Nor I Historickers," Creohan muttered. "Despite my one close friend, before you, being inclined to that. the swing, "where would he likely be—at the Houses of History?"

"I? Never!" The girl shivered visibly. "Did you ever meet anyone who managed merely to explore them, and not become trapped in their mazes of past time? I never did. It's as though our grip on the solid reality of now is so feeble that anything can drag people away from it: one whiff of that man's drugs, one step into the portals of a House of History . . . !"

"But we have a reason to resist that lure," Creohan said. "And if we're to find Glyre, we must venture thither. Come."

Overlooking the city on a gentle hill, the Houses of History stood in a vast bower of blue and green leaves. About their dark brown wall stretched lawns pleasant and soft in the sunlight, where Historickers in the clothes of half a hundred different ages stood, or sat, or lay, their eyes bewildered, their minds in tumult at the conflict between the vivid *then* and the dimly-perceived *now*. Back and forth Chalyth went among them, asking each about Glyre and the fallen city which had so entranced him and receiving always one of two responses: a blank smile with silence, or fierce boasting about some other period of history.

At length they addressed a boy not more than twenty years of age, whose reflexes seemed to be awaiting any outside trigger to operate. In him their questions provoked only movement. He rose unsteadily to his feet and looked about him, as though to convince himself beyond doubt of the worthlessness of the present moment, and headed straight for the nearest entrance to a House.

Chalyth and Creohan exchanged glances. Reaching their own common decision, they followed him, holding hands like frightened children venturing down a long dark corridor.

Over and over Molichant had explained to Creohan the presumed workings of the Houses of History, insofar as they were nowadays understood. The skills which had created them lay thousands of years in the past, at the limit of the Historickers' range, and had involved concepts very foreign to contemporary thinking. Nonetheless it was clear that in some fashion they caused currents in the mind, infinitely subtle, and memories lying below the cellular level, below the molecular, stored perhaps in some tenuous straining of the very fabric of the universe, emerged into awareness while one remained inside.

All these explanations, though, had ill-prepared Creohan for the reality that impinged on him when he crossed the threshold in the youth's wake. Abruptly, from one step to the next, his perception of even such fundamentals as the posture of his own body wavered and grew fluid; in the same instant as he took the next step, his limbs were not only walking, but running, lying at rest, spreadeagled on a wall and held with nails, lacking completely, bruised, caressed by gentle hands, burned, wrapped in smooth luxurious fabrics, stiff with age, disobedient with intoxicants . . .

He cried out, struggling to follow the youth ahead with his eyes, and saw him vanishing with decisive steps down a passage which was not a passage but a sequence of uncountably many different places: an open field, a dense forest, a waste of snow, a red city, a black city, a long grey road, a high stately banquet-hall, both separately and all at once. In the moment of looking, scores of images began to fight for the dominance of his brain, making him think of going insane.

Despite that, he forced himself forward, telling himself that only by exploring these passages could they hope to discover Glyre—there he was, that handsome black-skinned man with teeth filed into points, or else that shrivelled blond dwarf clad in badly-tanned hide, or—no, that was a woman, her face and bare breasts painted brilliant green, her lips purple and her eyes blank black hollows . . .

"No!" a voice said, and again, "No, no, no!" His hand, one of many, was tugged and he perforce followed the tugging, and the sluggish body he inhabited turned, and . . .

Clean sweet air, bright sun, green grass. He stared in disbelief, and grew eventually aware of the presence of Chalyth at his side, face pale with terror.

"Creohan, you cannot walk through there!" she whispered. "You're too much afraid of the future! The past has too much power over you!"

Rationality returned with a rush. He thought of what she had said, gave a sick nod, and bowed his head. Yes, that was something he should have been able to predict; his subconscious, full of terror at the future clashing of stars, would make him easy prey for the Houses of History, lacking even that self-control which enabled Historickers to choose what period they would permit to dominate their minds.

"We'll go then," he said. "We'll forget about Glyre and start into the world at random, and simply hope."

"Not so," Chalyth countered.

"What?"

"Look yonder," she said. "There, do you see a man in a golden helmet? It's exactly like the one my friend gave me under the sea. It must come from that same city. Almost I could believe that Earth herself is working on our side because our cause is worthy of her."

VI

THEY RAN PELL-MELL across the lawn, almost tripping over prostrate Historickers as they went. Yet their haste was unnecessary, for the old head of their quarry was bowed by the weight of the golden helmet and his clothes hung loose on a frame scrawny with age. His slow steps were directed towards the entrance of the nearest House of History, and he was still a dozen paces from his goal when they caught up to him.

"Sir!" Creohan panted. "Is not your name Glyre?"

The old man's bleary eyes turned towards him, finding apparent difficulty in focusing on anything in the present. "It is," he said rustily. "And why do you stop me thus?"

"To find out if you are that Glyre who made a great voyage across the sea and out of sight, many years ago."

The wrinkle-seamed face beneath the heavy helmet brightened, the bent back straightened pridefully. "That I am!"

"We want to talk with you about your journey, then," Chalyth said. "We want to know what you found."

40

"Wreckage and ruins," Glyre answered. "The merest, faintest shadow of a long-gone glory, that is all. And now if you'll excuse me . . ." He made to continue his approach to the House of History.

Seeking a way to delay the old man, Creohan gibed at that dormant but still existent pride. "So it comes to this, does it, that you who were once a man of spirit flee to the past like a frightened mouse heading for its hole?"

Unwounded, Glyre gave a creaking laugh. "What place is there in today's world for a man of spirit? What undertaking can engage his interest? If I could have found one, even one such man or woman as walked the streets of my dead city in its prime, I would perhaps have been content with life as it is. But I failed to find any. So"—he made a little empty gesture with one hand—"I, as you put it, fled."

"We plan an enterprise fit for a man of spirit," Chalyth said. "Sit down a while and we will tell you of it."

Reluctant, casting a longing eye towards the House of History, Glyre acknowledged that his legs were weak and consented to join them on a nearby bench. Briefly Creohan and Chalyth unfolded their intention to him, and when they were done he spoke in admiration.

"That is a noble project!" he exclaimed. "It is such as the people of the past used to undertake—people who did not know the meaning of the word 'impossible'. Would that you'd told me it a century ago, when I was young and vigorous and daring, for I'd have joined your company upon the instant! As it is"—he ruefully contemplated his withered right arm—"I shall soon be dead and fast forgotten. But you, if you succeed, will live on in the memories of all the men and women of Earth, instead of just the minds of those few Historickers who choose to enjoy your age.

"What small service I can perform for you, though, I will do happily, and that's to share with you knowledge which I had almost let slip my mind until I was listening to you talk just now. Ah, how it all comes back!" He clasped his hands before his chest and blinked up at the bright sky; then, as though remembering also why his head felt so burdened, he gingerly removed the helmet he wore and set it on his lap, stroking its fine engraved decoration with the tips of his fingers as he resumed.

"You see, I was not alone in my adventurousness. When I was a stripling there was a kind of fad for vain and perilous journeys, undertaken alone, as though I and my companions were seeking achievement in rivalry among ourselves. You knew my name, so you must have heard talk of me—but do you know the names of such as Breghinole, or Cazador, or Quace? No? Ah me!" A sigh racked him and threatened to become a cough, and for a moment he was lost in a silent struggle with his own reflexes. The impulse conquered, he went on again.

"That way walked Breghinole; he made to the north, along a strange winding road of some impervious rock, and found as he later told us curious deformed growths covering the land, that oozed a noxious sap and were unwholesome in the belly. Also among them went creatures he called wildmen, who could be heard jabbering after dark in unknown tongues. There he found tumbledown shacks of timber with the bark still on, laid out as though to make symbols of the reality of a house, in which the wildmen kept bees for the sake of their honey and at last when hunger tempted him to rob their stores he found how well they were guarded. A wildman smashed his elbow with a club, and he returned weak and ill and did not long survive. So in going north there seems to be no profit.

"No more is there in faring across the sea, as I myself did. Long days alone in my little open boat, with insufficient wind to fill the sail so that I burned with sun and parched for lack of sweet water—by all the ages, I must have been a crazy youth to torture my body so!—what did it gain me? I touched on islands that had once been great and prosperous, but where blank skulls now lie among the shattered fragments of high windows made of single jewels, broken by winter storms. There great grand towers, not grown of themselves like our houses here, but erected by the painful labour of men's hands, whistle hollow to the wind like organ-pipes and make lament for their vanished builders. I can hear that music still in my aging brain." Glyre put a palm to his temple, and winced. "The saddest sound in the world, my friends—the keening of mere objects for the loss of their owners!"

"But no one lives there?" Chalyth cried.

"Not merely *no one,*" the old man said. "No *thing,* either, except sprouts from seeds borne on the wings of the gale, that have lodged in dusty crevices and taken root. And those make funeral garlands, dark blue, mud-brown, or black."

Dismayed by this drab picture he conjured up for them, Creohan said, "What of the other travellers you mentioned that you knew? What of—was the name Cazador?"

"Yes, Cazador. And Quace. Well, as for *him,* he did not return. At least, not alive. Years after, when my own far journey was already dimming in my memory, I was walking on the beach some way from here at the point where the river they call Slaind meets the sea, when suddenly I saw a face peering at me from among the bushes which fledged the bank. I went in horror to see who was trapped there, for the person did not move, and—that was Quace. Wedged upright by large stones attached to his ankles with leather thongs, he was bobbing and swaying over elbows in the water, nodding back and forth and deriding the world with a fixed grin on his lips. Some message was cut into the bare skin of his chest, that was sodden and puffy, but I could not read the characters. Indeed, but for a ring he wore, which I recalled, I might not have known him as my friend."

"What happened to him?" Chalyth demanded.

"Oh, who can say? Perhaps some savages resented his intrusion in their domain, high up the course of the river he had informed us he would follow, and sent him back to the place he hailed from, dead, as a warning that none should come after. It was a long time ago, girl. A decade later I went to the spot again and there was nothing to be seen except a group of disorganised bones."

Chalyth and Creohan exchanged dismayed glances. They had not realised the world outside was so full of menace.

"And as for Cazador," Glyre continued, "why, he too may serve to warn you of a road you should not take. For he went east, and when he came back he was quite insane."

There was a long silence between them. During it, Creohan fancied he could feel the pulse and surge of the pattern of history, that at one time had dictated the rise of great empires and at another had decreed the collapse of the old to make room for the new. That pulse seemed to him to be slackening, like the passage of the blood in Glyre's old veins, and once more the fatalistic notion occurred to him that the onrush of the rogue star promised merciful release for the senile species, Man. But perhaps that was only the proximity of the House of History, evoking associations in his mind.

He said at last, "You've put up many barriers for us, Glyre!"

"Do not resent it!" said the old man, pleading. He put his bony hand on Creohan's knee. "Am I not doing a service as I promised? Am I not saving you from unknown dangers?"

"Of course you are," Chalyth said in a comforting tone. Unseen by Glyre, she gave Creohan a scowl.

"I would not have it otherwise," the old man said. "Until today I had thought nothing could tear my heart from the vanished people of my beloved dead city. But this I say in all sincerity: if it were possible, I'd forget them in order to come with you."

VII

SO, NEXT MORNING, they set forth in a direction which
Glyre's warnings had not closed to them, much burdened not merely with the tangible goods they foresaw
as needful, such as food and knives, but also with the
weight of apprehension his tales had created in their
minds. They went inland, away from the sea, until they
came to the place where the city blended almost imperceptibly into the green hills from which the meat came
nightly, shrieking its lunatic laughter.

The last house of all was a delicate bower, fresh and
flower-hung, and a girl sat in the doorway singing. She
had hair as yellow as sunlight and a voice like running
water.

"Pardon us, friend," said Creohan civilly. "Do you
know what lies beyond the hills ahead?"

The girl laughed. "No, stranger, I do not. I have sung
here for ten years, and I have never been further than
you can see. Is it not wonderful?"

"I call it craven-hearted," Chalyth responded bluntly,
and she and Creohan walked by.

They had gone only a few paces, though, when the

girl got up and came after them, crying for them to wait a while. Creohan turned and looked at her. She was very lovely, and she wore nothing but garlands of huge flowers picked from the walls of her house.

"What do you call us for?" he demanded.

"If you are in truth going over the hills, you may see a certain man who went that way a year ago. He is called Vence, and you may know him by his eyes: one's blue, the other's brown."

"So others *have* gone this way lately!" Chalyth burst out, and the girl dressed in yellow blossoms shook her head.

"One other, only one." Her lip trembled and her eyes began to fill. "Vence was my lover and we shared this house. We sang, we ate and drank, we made much love—what else was needed for us? And yet a year ago he went out to the hills and told me if I wanted him I could follow. I tried—in truth, I did try! But as I lost sight of the house my heart failed me, and I returned. Again I set out; again I had to abandon my intention. Ever since, I—I have been waiting." She blinked and spilled a tear into the upturned cup of one of the yellow flowers.

"What would you have us do, should we see this Vence?" Chalyth inquired.

"Tell him—tell him I'm still waiting," whispered the beflowered girl.

"We see that," Creohan said bluntly. "But what makes you think that he will be? If a man sets out on a journey, he does so with a purpose. I think he will not come back with that purpose unfulfilled. You will sit here growing old; those blossoms will wither and fall away, showing your naked body, how it is wrinkled and your breasts sag. Your voice will begin to crack on the high notes, your golden hair will tarnish with the dull heavy breath of time. Do you truly plan to wait for your man until he comes back and finds you—*old?*"

"Foul, foul!" the girl cried, and rounded on Chalyth. "Did you not hear the horrid things he said to me? How can you keep company with such a nasty man?" A thought struck her, and her tone changed to one of cajolement. "You should leave him before he turns the lash of his tongue on you! Why not take the chance before he drags you with him into wild and unknown lands? Come live with me here and sing in the sun before my door of flowers!"

There was no sympathy in Chalyth's face as she uttered her chill reply. "Perhaps you have never had a man who knew the value of truth. For myself, I'd rather go with one who can be honest than any of a thousand who can weave patterns of seductive lies."

"My Vence did not lie to me!" the girl bridled.

"Did you not promise him undying love?" Chalyth countered.

"Why—why, so I did, over and over."

"Then you were the liar between the two of you. You loved him so well you would not leave your home to accompany him." Chalyth's words were scathing. "Between me and Creohan there's not even a bond of love, only a shared purpose. So good day to you. We don't know where we're going, but it's likely to be a long way, so we can waste no more time."

"But you don't understand," the girl said miserably. "I ache for him with every cell of my body, and yet my mind is chained to my home. I could not go unless he dragged me, and because he loved me he would not do that . . . But—!" Her face suddenly brightened.

"You! You're strangers! *You* could force me to go! You could drive me onwards if I grew faint-hearted out of sight of my home! I do not want to sit here singing alone until I die, but without help I can do nothing else."

"Change your blossoms for warm clothing, then, and put strong shoes on your feet," Creohan answered. "We will not drag you, for that would slow us down, but until your heart fails again you may use our company for a crutch."

"So be it," said the girl in subdued tones, and went into her house to make ready.

"Was that wise?" said Chalyth in a low voice when she was gone, and Creohan shrugged.

"Since this whole enterprise is the very height of folly, what difference can one more piece of unwisdom make?"

The girl was long in coming back, so that Creohan and Chalyth began to suspect she had reconsidered her hasty decision. But when she did appear, she was clad in plain grey with shoes on her pretty feet; in her leather belt was thrust a knife, over her shoulder was slung a bag containing food, and from a baldric at her side there depended a little harp.

"Just so did my man set out," she said as she came near. "Except that he carried a flute instead of a harp. I am called Madal. And you?"

They told her, Creohan thinking that she must have more sense than he had given her credit for. Then they gave a last lingering glance back towards the city, though Madal's eyes went no further than her home.

"Onward," said Creohan, and they began to walk.

The sun passed the zenith and began to slide towards setting. At first they went on level turf; then they came to a stretch where the ground was rutted, in a pass between two hills, and after looking at the dints in the earth Creohan decided it must be by this route that the meat came nightly to the city. They picked their way delicately over the upturned dirt, agreeing to follow the tracks because they at least led somewhere.

Out of the corner of his eye Creohan noticed that Madal kept looking back, but he resolutely refused to copy her, even to see whether they were yet out of sight of her yellow home. Her face was set, and her mouth was frozen into a tight narrow line, but keeping level with her companions she plodded on.

The sun set and they were still following the track of the meat. By then Chalyth, the least burdened and most vigorous of the three of them, was leading the way at a cautious speed, a stick extended before her with which she thrust at soft-seeming patches of ground to warn the others of deep mud. Suddenly she halted and cried out.

"Listen!"

Far in the distance they could make out the crazy laughter of the meat as it wended its way towards a rendezvous with Death. Creohan looked about them. The light was dim and it was hard to make out details.

"We had best leave the track," he suggested. "I have never confronted a herd of meat on the move, but I imagine they would give us scant attention. That way looks easiest, towards the left."

They ran from the path up a steep slope, and perched on its grassy crown to wait for the meat to pass. The shrieking mirth grew louder and louder while the dusk deepened, until at length the leaders of the herd shambled into sight, shaggy and horrid in the gloom. Twice as high as a man, low-browed and lank-limbed, their vast padding feet squelching and plopping in the wet soil churned up by their passage, they made the very hills resound with the clamour of their manic delight: *hahaaa, hahaaa* . . . Creohan shuddered and had to cover his ears against the noise.

"I have never seen our meat alive before," said

Chalyth as the silence returned. "How like those beings are to men—two arms, two legs, an upright human stance! My stomach sours to think of them. Shall I ever be able to eat their flesh again?"

But Madal reacted differently. Her gaze fixed on the last point at which the meat had been in sight, she whispered, "They are going to our city! And in the morning when my neighbour calls for me to go together and fetch our bits of meat, he'll find my house empty and no clue to where I've gone. Tonight I shall lie out under the sky, when waiting there is the couch on which I've slept these ten years—alone of late, but not wishing it were so . . ."

Chalyth rounded on her. "Follow those beasts, then! These ten years that you have lain on your soft couch, I've slept under the sky, though I could have had my choice of a hundred beds. And I can go with a stranger on a grand vain quest, while you could not even tag at the heels of the man you claimed to love. Tag at *their* heels, then—those brutish unthinking clods treading the path their kind have trodden for centuries. We would rather make our own path, Creohan and I."

"You shame me," said Madal after a pause. "Even so did Vence shame me when he left and I could not follow. I do not like to be shamed. So be it—we sleep under the sky. Here? Or shall we trudge on until we drop with weariness?"

"No, here, I think," said Creohan, and sought a level place to stretch out upon. Chalyth broke branches from a low dry bush and built a fire, and they sat around it eating frugally of the provisions they carried, for they could not guess how long they must make their small store last.

Afterwards Madal took her harp and sang a sad slow song. She was still singing when Creohan and Chalyth fell asleep, and the melody rang through their dreams as though it were echoing from side to side of their skulls in the way the laughter of the herd of meat had rung between the hills.

The next morning they went on their way in silence, finding that they had almost reached the highest point of the area. For it was as yet well before noon when they breasted a rise—still following the track of the meat, which ran quite straight—and looked out over a plain rich with ripe yellow grasses.

It stretched as far as their eyes could see, and Chalyth murmured, "Now I can tell how Glyre felt when he launched out into the trackless ocean!"

"This is not trackless," said Creohan, and led the way scrambling down the abruptly sloping path. Thorny shrubs bordered it at this point, and caught on the sharp prickles were patches big as a man's palm torn from the grey-furred hide of the meat-creatures. Bloody stains testified to the eagerness with which they forced a way among the savage spikes. Creohan, half the size of one of those brutes, could himself barely thread his way between the clawing branches without being scratched; the giant beasts, struggling up the path two and three abreast in their haste, must be cruelly gashed by them, yet always and always they laughed . . .

Then the grasses were towering huge about them, their stems thick as his fingers. "Now we are compelled to follow the track," he muttered. "Otherwise we shall be lost. These stalks come higher than my head."

"That," Madal said tartly, "supposes that we're not lost anyway, and that the track leads somewhere."

"It must go, at least, to the place where the meat-creatures breed," Creohan pointed out. "And it's improbable that ours is the only city they supply with food. So there will be another track beyond the breeding-grounds, maybe several. Let's go ahead as quickly as we can."

Madal sighed, but settled her bag more comfortably on her shoulder and took the lead, thrumming a faint walking rhythm from the strings of her harp as though to lend herself courage. Falling into step behind her, Chalyth spoke to Creohan in a low voice.

"You saw the threatening star again last night?"

Creohan nodded. "Here where there are no lights flying we shall see it clearly every night."

"It must surely be my fancy—yet it seemed brighter already!"

To that he made no reply.

The trail wandered and twisted among the high grass. It was useless trying to strike away from it in a straight line, for the ground was so level it offered no points of vantage. Wearying, they walked until the sunlight no longer reached the ground between the ripe yellow vegetable walls enclosing them, and at that time they again heard the crazy laughter of approaching meat.

"Of course, the nearer we get to their breeding-ground the earlier in the day we shall encounter them," Creohan reasoned, as they rounded a bend in the track.

Beyond, the way abruptly straightened for a hundred and fifty paces, and rounding another curve at the far end of the straight stretch they saw the herd confronting them. Somehow by daylight the beasts looked both more and less like men, and they laughed—how they laughed! A blind panic seized Madal, and she turned incontinently and ran.

"Get off the track, you fool!" shouted Creohan. Without waiting to see if she complied, he seized Chalyth by the arm and parted the grass to let them through. Hidden, they panted out of sight as the herd tramped by, the thick stems springing back to the vertical and concealing them.

After the sound of the laughter faded Creohan made to return to the track, but Chalyth begged him to wait for fear there might be laggards bringing up the rear of the herd. He consented worriedly, wondering whether Madal had fled blindly down the path or whether she had managed to hide among the grass as they had done. Their answer came soon.

"Creohan! Chalyth!" It was a high frightened call. "I'm lost! I can't find my way back to the track!"

They exchanged alarmed glances. "You cannot be far off," Creohan shouted back. "We hear you clearly. Can you not see the stems you bent when you left the path?"

Chalyth touched his arm and silently indicated the grass they themselves had pushed aside. Except where their weight still bowed it, it revealed no trace of their passage.

"Stay where you are, Madal!" Creohan cried again when he realised the truth. "Call out every now and then, and we will head towards you."

"She appears to be in that direction," Chalyth said, pointing. "Maybe she turned off the track on the other side from us, in which case we'll stumble across it as we go."

"Agreed," said Creohan, and forged his way ahead.

But the tough stems kept turning them imperceptibly aside from their course. Terror increased in Madal's frantic calls, and when they at last heard her very close and thrust aside the grass and saw her, she was crouched on her knees with her face buried in her hands. When she looked up her cheeks were wet with tears.

"Where is the trail?" she moaned. "Where can it have gone?"

"We did not cross it while we were finding you," Chalyth admitted.

"Then we are lost!" Madal wept. "We shall starve to death among these accursed plants!"

"Nonsense," said Creohan. "At least, the next time some meat passes, we shall hear them and head in their direction."

"I have a faster trick than that," Chalyth declared. "Bow your back, Creohan, and I will stand on it and look about."

Amazed he had not thought of that himself, he bent, and she scrambled up nimbly. "Well," Madal demanded, "do you see the trail?"

"I see something of greater interest," Chalyth replied. "I see smoke, rising from someone's fire!"

"You are certain?" Creohan was so startled he all but straightened and sent her flying.

"It's definitely smoke, and I doubt that the meat-creatures would build fires. These stems would catch light easily, too—were it a wild fire we'd already be trapped. It must be burning in a cleared space, and supervised."

VIII

STILL SNUFFLING, MADAL followed them as they forced a way among the high tough grass, pausing every now and then to let Chalyth climb up again and take a fresh bearing. Shortly, however, they could be in doubt of their goal no longer, for the distinct pungent reek of smoke came to them, accompanied by a faint noise. Finally they emerged into a trampled clearing twenty-odd paces wide, and stared in amazement to see a sort of crude shelter made of plaited grass-stems, propped up with what at first appeared to be white branches, but proved on closer examination to be long dry bones.

Now it was not only the odour of smoke they discerned in the air. Underlying it was another, less palatable smell, compounded of spilt blood and singeing hair. The source of the buzzing became obvious. One of the meat-creatures, gutted and flayed, lay lacking an arm at the far edge of the cleared area, and the exposed flesh was crawling with noisy flies.

The limb itself was scorching above the fire, on a sort of trivet likewise made of bones—a material of which there was no shortage here, for a knee-high stack of

them, many still bearing shreds of flesh through which
maggots burrowed, lay beside the shelter. A man sat
watching the meat cook with such concentration that
he hardly moved his shaggy head to acknowledge the
newcomers' intrusion on his solitude. Irresolute, Creohan walked close to him and spoke.

"Friend, do you know where the path leads to that
runs across this plain?"

The man's hair and beard were so tangled together
that his head seemed to be a ball of whiskers. His
body was filthy, and if he had ever owned clothes they
had long ago worn to shreds. Now he opened his eyes
wide and looked at Creohan, who started, for one of
those eyes was blue and the other brown.

"No path goes anywhere across this plain," the man
said rustily, and went back to staring at his food.
Creohan glanced at Madal, but it was plain she had not
recognized this unclean wretch. She was wandering
about with a look of mingled fascination and repug-
nance, peering into the shelter, examining the heap of
bones. Hoping that the shock would not overwhelm
her, he spoke harshly.

"So this is the sorry end of your bold journey,
Vence!"

The man leapt to his feet. In the same instant Madal
whirled, stared, let out a sighing gasp and might have
fallen had not Chalyth stepped hastily to her side and
caught her arm before echoing Creohan's last word
incredulously.

"Vence? You mean this *thing* is Madal's lost lover?"

"Well?" Creohan pressed the stranger. "Are you
not truly he?"

Wilting under the burning stare, the man gave a
sullen nod. "Yes, that's what I was called. And there
is Madal with you yonder. I had—forgotten her name—
until your woman spoke of it."

"What happened to you?" Creohan demanded. "What are you doing here? How do you live? And *why?*"

"Live?" said Vence sourly. "This is not living, this is mere existence. The days melt together like coloured wax until they blend in a grey featureless nothingness." He gestured at the roasting meat as though to excuse himself for failure. "I do have food, though. Should I—ah—give you some?"

"But why are you here alone?" Creohan cried, ignoring the repulsive offer. "Why did you end your trip so close to home?"

"Close? *Close?* I don't know if you're a liar or a fool or the spawn which the sun has finally bred in my brain! I was driven off the pathway by a herd of meat, and I tramped this horrible plain for thirty days, up and down and around. For thirty long dreadful days I *know* I went forward, until by chance I stumbled once more across a track used by the meat-creatures and realised I must remain close to it or starve. At least I've stayed alive." Once more he pointed to the meat. "Look—smell! Is it not fresh and good?"

Creohan tried to keep his eyes from wandering to the flies which swarmed on the new-dead carcase. He said, "And you're content to sit here, on this one spot you've so befouled? Do you no longer want anything else of life?"

Vence shrugged and squatted on his haunches again, his dour self-possession seeming to return. "What else did I ever have from life except sitting in one place the whole day long?"

"But—but how do you overcome the meat you kill? You're surely not strong enough to drag a brute like that with your bare hands all the way from . . ."

By the way of answer Vence tugged up the hilt of a

knife, whose blade he had buried in the dirt at his feet
to rub off the blood.

"That's a puny weapon," Creohan said. Vence's
upper lip curled in a derisory grin as he sank the knife
back into the ground.

"Ah, the beasts are near enough human in some
ways, and you can use a little guile with them. Fair
words and certain acts will bring them willingly. Look
there, look close. You'll see my prize is female." He
seemed to take a relish in boasting of his degradation.
"All my prizes are female. And they can be made to
serve a man's desires. Isn't that all one ever needs a
female for?"

What happened next occurred so fast that Creohan,
taken aback, could not follow it while it was going on,
but had to reconstruct it afterwards. A frantic movement, a wild flailing of something long and white, a
cracking noise, a scream—and there was Madal, face
transfigured with fury, standing over the whimpering
body of her former lover and shaking at him the long
thigh-bone she had brought slamming like a hammer
against the side of his head.

"You brute! You beast! You less than animal *thing!*"
she screeched. "Was that all you ever found to like in
me, who loved you and waited on you and wept to see
you leave? I hate you, hate you, *hate* you, do you
hear?"

She began to belabour him frantically with the heavy
bone. On one hand and two knees he tried to scuttle
sideways and reach his knife, with the other hand vainly
trying to fend off the blows she rained on him: shoulder, back, scalp, thigh, each with the full violence of
her rage behind the impact. Creohan and Chalyth tried
to restrain her, but she bared her teeth at them and
threatened to strike them also if they interfered.

"Do I not owe him this for stealing ten precious years of my life?" she forced out. "The dirty liar! To think he could have used me like—like one of *those!*" She jabbed the bone through the air in the direction of the flayed carcase. Vence whimpered aloud.

But he must have been less dazed than he appeared, for in the next moment he had hurled himself sideways, rolling, his mouth opening to bite at Madal's calf. An early blow, however, had injured it—just how, the matted tangle of his beard prevented Creohan from seeing—and when he moved the muscles of his jaw the pain was so great he howled, forgot his weak attempt at retaliation, and sat there rocking back and forth and wringing his hands.

"Leave him be," Chalyth ventured. "His long loneliness has turned his brain; he will never be a proper man again."

"No!" Madal flared. "I'll make use of him, I swear I will! Did he not claim to know in which direction the path lay? Then he can lead us to it, at the very least. *Come* on, you stinking manure-pile!" She delivered another vicious jab at Vence's back, and he forced himself wavering to his feet.

"Do you think it's safe to leave this fire?" Chalyth asked, with a doubtful glance at the tall dry grass around them.

Vence moaned, eyes rolling, but the words would not pass his injured jaw in clear language.

"I think he wants it left alight," Madal interpreted. "In which case—you're right, aren't you? Cover it with dirt and let's be gone!"

With the tips of his fingers Creohan stirred the piled bones until he came on a flat shoulderblade, which he used to dig up a few scoops of soft earth. The fire died, hissing. Madal checked Vence's attempt to prevent the act with a kind of vicious satisfaction.

"Now, take us to the trail!" she snapped at last.

He turned and broke into a stumbling trot, following a line along which the grass-stems parted very readily, and Madal hurried at his heels, lashing him on with the bone for a goad. Creohan and Chalyth had all they could do to keep up. At last they came to the track again, the broad clear gap in the grass where it was trampled flat so often by the meat it had no chance to grow to normal height—and Vence seemed not to see it, but dashed straight ahead and was immediately lost among the grass on the other side.

"Good riddance!" Madal exclaimed, panting. She leaned on the bone like a staff and glowered at the stalks which now were springing back to the vertical.

Arriving at her side, Chalyth said, "You're going to let him go? You're going to leave him to starve with a broken jaw here in the wilderness?"

"He left me to eat out my heart with longing," Madal said with contempt. "I'm doing no more than setting the account to rights."

"Whatever he did to you," Chalyth said obstinately, "with a broken jaw he'll starve! And we who are seeking a way to save the lives of people yet unborn should not so lightly condemn the people of the present to a lingering death!"

"Lightly?" Madal echoed. "Ten stolen years, and you say I do this lightly? Oh, go after him then—for all I know you're fit company for the dirty brute!"

But the fierceness of her rage was leaking away, and in one more instant she had let the bone fall and stumbled blindly to the comfort of Chalyth's arms, her slim frame racked with sobbing.

"It's horrible, it's horrible!" she wept. "I did love him, truly I did, and he was kind and thoughtful and he played the flute so well!"

"We don't doubt it," Creohan said. "It must indeed

be that long loneliness has broken down his mind. That's not your Vence who's fled into the sea of grass, but another in his body, who has become much less than a man."

"Even so, should we not save him from that awful fate?" Chalyth said. "Starving because he cannot bite his food?"

"I think it would do no good," Creohan sighed. "You've seen how hard it is to spot someone among this grass, and we were only looking for Madal, who was waiting in the same spot. To pursue someone who is trying to get away would be fruitless, and we ourselves might never find the trail again."

"I guess you're right," Chalyth said after a pause. "But . . . Well, there's no help for it, I must agree. So what will you do, Madal—turn and head for home?"

The yellow-haired girl wiped away her tears. She said, "I think I'd rather find a reason to go on. Going back on my own, who's to say I might not suffer the same fate as Vence? He was a strong good man once, I swear he was! But equally what profit lies in going forward? There was one of him and we are three; three times as far from home as he reached, will we become like him?"

"No, we have a purpose," Creohan declared. "Vence must have left home from simple restlessness, and in the end found he had not enough knowledge of himself to discover a purpose for his travels. But we set out for a very pressing reason."

"To save the world?" Madal gave a sarcastic laugh. "One man, one woman, to divert a star?"

"No, that's not the thing that drives us," Chalyth said with naked honesty. "The truth is—we're afraid."

"Of what? A disaster that will happen when you're both long dead?"

"I know what makes me fearful," Chalyth said. "The

world is so large, and I so small, and I may die before I understand a tithe of it. You, Creohan?"

"Yes, I'm afraid," Creohan admitted. "Though I may be forgotten by choice on the part of those who come after us, I do not wish that there should be no one at all who might choose to remember me. And you, Madal? Have you a fear that will make you continue in our company?"

"If fear will serve for reason," Madal said at length, "you already know the answer. I'm afraid to go back alone. So I'll go on. Which way, Creohan?"

Creohan glanced up at the sun and calculated. "That way," he said, and began to stride determinedly along the path again.

IX

LATE IN THE day the ground across which the path was leading them began to take an upward turn, and the nature of the vegetation altered. Among the grass, which was here scattered in clumps a few feet wide, there appeared shrubs with pale blue flowers, thick-boled miniature trees not as high as Creohan with peculiar stiff leaves that tinkled against each other, and groups of colossal puffballs as translucent as frog-spawn. Something could be dimly seen inside each ball, but they found that they preferred not to examine the contents too closely; the shapes were disquieting.

Madal, it seemed, would not have been distracted by a lightning strike at her feet, so depressed was she after their encounter with Vence. She went in silence, eyes fixed on the path, and her companions respected her desire to be left in peace. However, they talked between themselves as they walked, for they were already seeing many strange things.

"Creohan, how is it that plants can change so rapidly?" Chalyth demanded, having plucked one of the blue flowers to sample its odour, and, dismayed, seen it turn rotten-brown on the instant. "We've not moved to another climatic zone, yet I've never seen such growths around our home city. Is it some shift in the nature of the soil?"

"That may contribute," Creohan replied. "But this is a matter I once discussed with Molichant, and he told me it was a testament to the fantasy of man— that a thousand centuries of meddling with them and letting them be by turns produced this incredible variety of plants."

Astonished, Chalyth gestured at one of the clumps of puffballs they were passing. "But what conceivable purpose could anyone have in creating a species like that—if it is indeed artificial?"

"Maybe there was no purpose." Creohan shrugged. "Maybe there was only curiosity. Most likely, though, there was a purpose which to us now is inaccessible. We seem to have invented many improbable goals for ourselves. When I think of the way the Gerynts . . ." He swallowed hard. "Well, that woman who attacked me in the tavern, as I described to you: I find it impossible to understand her motivation, yet she was a citizen of our own age."

"Contaminated," Chalyth said.

"Yes."

There was a pause. During it, he glanced back to see if Madal was still keeping up and realised that now the slope had carried them high enough to see the yellow grassy plain like a sea, its surface rippling to the touch of a breeze. Nothing further away could be discerned; haze masked the horizon and blended the juncture of earth and sky into a vague shimmer of blue.

"Creohan," Chalyth said, "something puzzles me. Do you see anything odd about this section of the road?"

"Odd?" Creohan echoed, and stared ahead and around. It was a moment before he hit on what she was referring to, but then he was surprised at not having seen it for himself. Up till now the track made by the meat had never been straight for more than a hundred paces or so at one time, but it had always gone roughly in the same direction, curving a few degrees this side, a few that, and maintaining its general course by average.

Along this stretch, however, it was distinctly zigzag, with unprecedentedly sharp angles at frequent intervals, and there were rather steep banks on either side.

Creohan stopped. Behind him Madal did the same, her face blank of any reaction. Taking a knife from his pack, he tried to drive the point into the bank nearest him, and met resistance an inch below the surface. He tried elsewhere, with the same result, then scraped away the masking vegetation and threw it down.

Revealed was the face of a large polished stone, with a crack running corner to corner and the hair-fine tendrils of fungal mycelia threading out of it. Some insects, fearing light, scuttled for shelter before he could see what they were.

"I thought so," Chalyth said softly. "Where we stand, Creohan, was there not once a city of the ancient style, with man-made walls instead of self-grown houses?"

"There must have been," Creohan agreed, and shook his head in wonder. "And no trace of it remains visible, except the sketched line of those straight streets that the meat-creatures have chosen to follow, making the nearest approach they could to a direct course across the site."

"It's a fearful thought," Chalyth muttered. "How can Historickers bear to delve into the past, knowing what fate overtook the builders, the inventors, the rulers and the common folk?"

"Perhaps it gives them a sense of superiority, being

still alive themselves," Creohan answered cynically. "Despite the evidence with which the world is littered, I think few men—or women either—can honestly believe the inevitability of death."

He sheathed his knife, and concluded, "Anyway, I suspect we've hit on the reason for the sudden change in the nature of the plants around here. As you proposed, there's a change in the nature of the ground. Possibly the folk who built this city liked to have things like these monstrous puffballs growing in their gardens."

"Monstrous is an apt term," Chalyth said. "Have you noticed that one, looming up ahead past the next corner?" She pointed, and Creohan looked where she indicated. He saw a vast swollen bubble, so over-taut that it seemed on the verge of bursting, strained to such transparency that it was only detectable against the air thanks to the glint of the declining sun on its exterior. And the dark shape inside was moving.

Creohan felt a pang of irrational alarm, but told himself brusquely that the motion must be due to the breeze. He gestured for them to continue forward, taking the lead and setting a brisk pace. Drawing closer to the giant puffball, however, his feet slackened without intention. There was something about that all too clearly visible form which made the hairs rise prickling on his nape.

"Hurry, Creohan!" Chalyth urged. "Let's pass that thing as quickly as we can."

Relieved to know his alarm was shared, Creohan complied, keeping to the side of the path further from it, for its vast dilated bulk was trespassing down the bank and in a short while would probably bar the way completely. Reflexively he reached behind him for Chalyth's hand, and murmured that she should take

Madal's, there being irrational comfort against irrational fears in the simple contact of skin.

He drew level with the puffball and began to sidle, for a strange desire possessed him to see the shape within. He made out that there must be fluid as well as gas inside, for there was a roiling of dull yellow-grey matter near the base, and it was from the middle of this that the central form protruded. A sort of irregular dome, with two dark pits beneath, and then another pit like an inverted half-moon, and barely above the level of the yellow-grey substance a horizontal slit with indistinct whitish vertical bars crossing it. The whole was about half as high as himself, so that with the bank to raise it above the path the dark pits were on a level with his eyes—

Eyes?

In the same instant as himself, Chalyth recognised the object's true shape, disguised until now by its excessive size, and cried aloud.

"Oh, Creohan, it's a *face!*"

As though the words were a signal, the covering of the twin dark pits split raggedly and fell in drifting flakes to the roiling fluid at the base. Revealed were two huge white staring orbs each with a dark vertical slit. They were confronted with a hideous inhuman gaze that froze them to the spot.

The head tilted back, and the whitish bars were exposed as teeth, great spiky fangs with liquid dripping from their tips, and Creohan recovered the power to move. He dragged Chalyth away, and she Madal, both stumbling, for some ten paces. There a large rock lying loose on the ground caught his eye; he let go Chalyth's hand, seized the lump of stone, whirled and flung it with all his force at the bulging membrane of the puffball.

It gashed the upper surface, and instantly the gas

within began to leak away, causing a high sighing moan, a vegetable cry of despair. The ballooning globe collapsed inwards, wrinkled, became opaque as it dwindled, and finally draped like a grey shroud around the horrible head. They stood in silence until they were sure it was inert.

Then Chalyth passed her hand across her forehead wearily. *"That* was no natural plant!" she said. "But what incredible twisted human mind could conceive it, let alone actively desire its existence?"

"I don't know and I don't care," Creohan grunted. "All I want is to get out of the region where these horrors grow. Madal, are you all right—? Why, girl! Your feet are stained with blood!"

Indeed, there were reddish marks on both of Madal's shoes.

"We'll go on," she said dispiritedly. And, when the others wavered, she added in a fiercer tone, "I said go on! I too want to leave this area, sore feet or no!"

Doubtfully, Creohan offered to take her burdens from her, but she refused the offer with a curt head-shake and strode away, face very white, lips pressed together as though to repress a moan of pain. Accepting her decision, the others followed her.

Not long after their way began to slope upwards more sharply than ever, so that they were compelled to go slowly and seek handholds for fear of slipping. But once more the vegetation had changed, with no more of the strange puffballs or blue-flowered shrubs. Instead, they encountered purple moss and dull lichens clinging to otherwise naked rocks; here and there a red-leaved tree made obscene gestures at the sky with its branches. It was approaching sunset, and Creohan was minded to suggest finding a place to camp, when all of a sudden he heard a noise at the edge of audibility.

"Listen!" he said, halting and raising one hand. "Is that not the laughter of the meat?"

"I think it is," Chalyth confirmed after a moment. "But there's so much of it!"

Creohan studied the lay of the nearby land, and snapped his fingers. "I think we must be close to the breeding-ground," he announced. "Look how this hill we're climbing forms a curve. Beyond I foresee a valley shaped like a bowl, and we hear the laughter reflected by the hard rocks enclosing it."

"Quick then! To the top!" And Chalyth scrambled upwards more vigorously than ever. She, of course, was used to fighting ocean currents in the dark and the exercise had made her body as tough and supple as a good sword-blade. Creohan, on the other hand, was beginning to be amazed at the way his own body had answered his demands, and feared to wear himself out. He came up more slowly, lending Madal a hand over the most difficult sections of the climb.

Ahead, Chalyth vanished between two boulders. In a moment her cry came back urging them to join her.

"You were right, Creohan. This is—enormous!"

There was indeed a bowl-shaped valley beyond the hill. It was not very deep, but it was wide, and they could not see the other side of it because a huge weathered hump rose in the middle. Creohan looked at the way the hills were piled up about them, like mud splashed by a blow from a hammer, and remembered certain features on Mercury which had passed into the field of his telescope. So interested did he become at the realisation that he was on the lip of a meteoritic crater that he almost forgot to look at the hordes of meat which roamed its floor, tearing ripe white chunks from the stem of a kind of cactus which grew everywhere in clumps. They gobbled with feverish ecstasy, as if dimly aware that the more they ate the sooner would they be fat and ready to be themselves eaten.

"You are they who have been despoiling my flock," said a voice behind them harshly. "Deny it if you dare!"

They swung around. Facing them from an overhang of rock was what at first looked like one of the meat-creatures; in fact, it was a man of ordinary stature, who had taken the whole hide, grey fur and all, from one of the brutes and after shortening the limbs had tied it round himself. His muscular arms held taut the string of a bow, and the arrow nocked to it looked sharp enough to pierce all three of them at once.

X

"YOU HAVE BEEN robbing me!" the man shouted. "Prepare to die!"

"No, no!" Creohan exclaimed, and added with sudden inspiration: "The one who has been robbing you is wandering in the plain of yellow grass, his jaw so injured that he cannot eat!"

"See for yourself if we have taken any of your meat," Chalyth chimed in, unslinging her bag and opening it to display what little provision still remained to her. Cautiously, to avoid alarming the aggressive stranger, the others copied her.

"Indeed I see you have no meat," the man agreed at length, sounding puzzled. But he lowered his bow. "Where do you come from, and why are you here?"

"We come from the city which lies yonder, over the plain and close beside the sea," Creohan replied, and pointed as nearly as he could judge by the sun in the correct direction.

The effect of these few words on the skin-clad man was quite astonishing. Abruptly he let fall his bow, hid his face in his hands, and wept uncontrollably.

72

Forgetful of her wounded feet, Madal looked about for a way to reach the outcrop on which the man stood. Finding no path, she seized the brink of the rock and swung herself up by main force.

"What ails you, my poor fellow?" she said tenderly. "What makes you cry?"

The man snuffled like a huge baby, so that his reply emerged in fits and starts punctuated by racking gasps of air.

"You—you come from a city—and you have no meat—it can all have—only one meaning! We have failed! My brothers and I have failed!"

"How, failed?" Madal pressed him, stroking his thick unkempt hair with gentle hands.

Recovering himself, the man spoke more normally, but still shielded his face as though ashamed to confront them openly.

"We devote our lives to watching over our herds, and we send them out in due time to all the various cities, as our fathers taught us and their fathers taught them and so to the beginning of time. Once, very long ago, strangers did come to us, to tell us they had no meat, so we had failed. And here you are, and you too have no meat!"

"But there is meat at our city," Madal declared. "It comes daily from the hills and all who desire it have enough and to spare."

The man's face changed like sunlight breaking through a stormcloud. "That's the truth?" he demanded, wiping his eyes with the shaggy hair of his sleeve. Yet he still seemed doubtful. "Why have you none of it for your journey, then?"

Creohan spoke up, reasoning that to inform someone whose entire life was dedicated to raising the herds of meat for the sake of unseen distant cities about the ability of modern houses to feed their occupants without recourse to animal flesh would be unwise.

"We did not bring more with us than we needed to reach this place. What could be more pointless than to bring meat here, where there's so much of it?"

The man stared at him, eyes large and round. Suddenly he began to chuckle, then chortle, then pant and whoop with laughter as crazy as the meat-creatures' own. Jumping to his feet he performed a dance of joy, and all but tried to run up the sheer side of a nearby boulder.

"Come then! Come with me to my brothers! We must make a feast, a great big feast that will last all night long! Oh, but there will be such excitement at the news—we didn't fail, we didn't fail!" He broke off, and came to address Chalyth and Creohan over the outcrop's edge. Mercurially his mood had changed again and he seemed half angry.

"But why could you not have done this before? Was there too much to be done in your far-off city for you to spare the time to think of us? My father lived out his life and died without once discovering whether he had done his task well or ill. I have often thought I ought to go out in the wake of one of the herds which we daily drive forth, follow them to a city and *ask* if we've done well. But there's so much work to share among so few of us . . . Oh, what am I up to, friends, to complain to you who came all this way just to bring the very news we craved?"

"Well, as a matter of fact—" Chalyth began. Creohan silenced her with a glare.

Noticing nothing amiss, the herdsman bent to retrieve his fallen bow, and in so doing saw Madal's bloodstained shoes.

"Why, you have hurt yourself for our sake!" he

exclaimed. "You must walk no more until you're healed. I'll carry you to our home."

And, cradling the girl in his arms without effort, he leapt from the overhanging rock and led the way downhill. Following, Chalyth murmured under her breath to Creohan, "Did you imagine there were such people as he in the world?"

Creohan almost laughed. "The world is so much greater and stranger than I ever dreamed, I here and now resolve not to be surprised at anyone we may encounter. Hope only that they who live on the road we've chosen are all as reasonable as our herdsman friend, rather than like the savages who slaughtered Quace."

At the mention of Glyre's comrade a shadow crossed Chalyth's face, and they went on in silence.

They headed directly across the valley's floor, and shortly found themselves among a browsing herd of meat, who stopped eating at their master's approach and came shambling up to him. He called them each by name, and spared one hand from his burden to slap their buttocks or scratch their hairy coats, and they laughed their demonic laugh and moved away. Creohan wondered how many names the herdsman had to know to keep track of his beasts, and how it felt to send creatures so like himself off to their deaths each day.

The "home" he had spoken of proved to be a cave hollowed out from the central massif. Its only lighting came from wicks afloat in dishes of tallow; the stink of their burning hardly overcame the powerful reek of human occupation. Their wan flames revealed that the rock was seamed with metallic veins, smoke-dulled but distinctive, and Creohan was more than ever sure that this could only be a vast meteorite that had crashed here in the far past. Possibly it was the celestial hammerblow of its arrival that had laid low the city they had passed through earlier in the day. He wondered if he would ever again return to the Houses of History so that he might make inquiries about the matter among the Historickers of home.

There was no furniture except for shelves and niches carved in the rock itself, but there were large piles of skins near the mouth of the cave, and a big fire smoked to ward off the evening chill.

"Wait here," their host instructed. "I go to inform my brothers." He made to lay Madal down on one of the piles of skins, and his face registered enormous surprise—as did those of the others—when he discovered she had fallen asleep with her head against his chest. She barely stirred as he lowered her, but gave a wriggle and pressed her cheek into the yielding furs.

He explained that his brothers were out detailing the herds due to be sent forth at first light on the morrow. Puzzled by an elementary question of biology, Creohan asked whether he had sisters as well, but the word seemed to mean nothing to him.

"One thing further," Chalyth said, before the herdsman went off. "Have you a name?"

"Of course!" the man cried. "You are strangers here, and I'm not known to everyone in the world as I am throughout this valley. Hey!" he shouted to a group of meat-creatures grazing not far from the cave-mouth. "Name me!"

As one the beasts threw back their heads and bellowed, "Arrheeharr!"

"You see?" the man said. "When one comes among us who has not got a name, we show him to the meat, and the first name they give that we do not have already, that is his."

Then his excitement overcame him, and he departed at a wild run.

Creohan moved to spread his hands before the fire,

keeping his head down to avoid the drifting smoke. "Well?" he said to Chalyth. "Do you think these people can set us on the trail to another city?"

"He spoke of cities in the plural," Chalyth answered. "I have the impression, though, that their whole universe is bounded by this valley. For all our friend's remarks about not going to see what was becoming of his meat because there was so much work to be done and so few to share it, I rather suspect he was a victim of the same trouble as Madal—afraid to wander out of sight of home."

"Don't speak too harshly of her," Creohan reproved. "Did you not feel, when he broke out crying and she climbed up to comfort him, that there was a tenderness in her seeking a purpose she could put it to?"

"I did," Chalyth admitted. "And because of it I think I could despise Vence with the same force as she does."

"It's ironical that our venture to save mankind should begin under the shadow of so much suffering," Creohan muttered. "The thought of him starving with a broken jaw is going to haunt my nights."

"It's no good worrying about the past," Chalyth said. "We can't amend it. It's only the future we can hope to control. And passing through that abandoned city-site today, I found myself wondering what good the attempt is anyhow. Our planet is littered ankle-deep with the relics of vanished peoples."

"True enough," Creohan agreed. "Some may be crushed flat beneath this very spot—this rock, if I'm correct, is a meteorite, fallen out of the sky."

"Never!" said Chalyth in wonderment, and turned to stare at the monstrous looming mass. "Well, if the people who went before could not save themselves from that, what chance have we to save Earth from colliding with a star?"

"I don't know," Creohan sighed. "One thing I'd not appreciated fully before we set forth, and that's how empty our modern world must be. I learned of that, like so much else, while talking to Molichant at home; he said there had several times been many billions of us. Perhaps we're reduced to a handful because our time has come."

"So soon?" Chalyth exclaimed.

"Soon? Is it soon? It's been generally agreed for millennia that we first learned to handle tools and light ourselves fires two million years ago. That's a shortish span for a species, but not by any means the shortest known."

There was a silence. Eventually Chalyth said in a brighter tone, "We're still too close to home to consider such gloomy ideas. Let's change the subject. Tell me: how do you think these meat-creatures, so like men, have become nothing but food?"

"Might it not be the other way around? Who knows how long these brothers have guarded their herds in this valley? Is it not possible that over the generations the animals have grown to be more like men than formerly?"

"If they can change in that fashion, then who is to say when they have become too much like men to be slaughtered for their meat? Vence said the females were near enough human for . . ." She choked on the words, and gave a shiver. But Creohan wasn't listening anyway. He was staring up into the gathering dusk.

"Look there," he said. "The threatening star is showing in the sky."

XI

WHOOPING AND SHOUTING very like that of the meat-creatures but not so shrill disturbed them. Madal stirred and sat up. Through the twilight they saw Arrheeharr and his brothers approaching, bounding from hillock to hillock in their joy. There were eight of them, clad as he was in undressed skins; one bore the carcase of a freshly-killed animal on his back, another had a child of a few summers trotting at his heels. They clustered about Chalyth and Creohan asking eager questions, exclaiming in amazement at their clothing and belongings, and demanding confirmation of what Arrheeharr had told them.

"Yes, I can assure you," Creohan declared over and over, "never once in all my life in the city I hail from did I hear a word of complaint about the way you attend to your work, and I'm only sorry that no one has come to tell you so before."

That delighted them more than ever, and they fell to preparing their feast. One stoked the fire, one began to flay the carcase, a third plumped up the piles of skins. Watching them, Creohan saw the answer to his earlier puzzlement; it was evident through the gaps in the front of the skins they wore that these "brothers" were in fact of both sexes—four and four, with the child a boy. Perhaps in this life where all must work and act alike, the distinction between "he" and "she" had somewhere been lost. Certainly they were all as muscular and tough-looking as Arrheeharr regardless of their gender.

He noticed other points which struck him as significant. They were crudely clad and shaggy-haired, but none of them was dirty, and after dealing with the messy task of carving up their meat the butcher in charge went around the side of the meteorite-hillock and came back dripping with fresh water, all traces of blood washed away. There must be a spring or a well back there, he deduced. They had only the simplest tools, many of them—like Vence's—made of bone, but when one of them laid a knife down within his reach and he had a chance to examine it, he found its haft was decorated with an engraved drawing of a meat-creature, skilfully executed. Oh yes: these herdsmen, unbelievably inbred, isolated completely from the greater world, had somehow contrived to remain human.

Wondering at the unlikeliness of it all, he stared around him and realised that while he was studying his hosts, one of them was busy studying him. Standing a little apart was a man no taller than Chalyth, with a nervous, intense air, in whose dark-browed face Creohan read exceptional intelligence. Thinking back, he realised that this man alone of the herders had refrained from joining in the general excitement their arrival had caused, and had stood a little apart, seeming thoughtful, his dark eyes posing unspoken questions which, Creohan felt, he would find it impossible to answer.

"Hoo!" called Arrheeharr from a spot near the fire,

and the dark man turned his head slowly. "Hoo, fetch liquor from the store, won't you? We mustn't stint our guests, after all!"

A ghost of a smile touched the dark one's lips, but he departed into the depths of the cave without comment. While he was gone, Creohan's attention was caught by Madal, who on waking had struck up an instant friendship with the little boy and was now coming with him to join the group working at the fire. The clumsiness with which they were going about their task seemed to irritate her. Hoping that they did not all share the mercurial touchiness of Arrheeharr, Creohan watched as she prepared a crude stone oven for the meat, so that it might bake instead of being scorched on a spit, and sent for juicy roots and leaves to flavour it while it was cooking. Arrheeharr fetched her bag at her request, and from it she took salt and other condiments, so that a rich and appetising smell soon went up, causing gasps of astonishment from their hosts.

"That's good," said a soft voice by Creohan's side. "I was half afraid she might offend them by taking charge."

He glanced around and discovered Chalyth at his elbow. "Yes, so was I," he agreed. "Hope only that she's not so successful at gaining their favour that they try to prevent us leaving again!"

At that moment Hoo returned with a barrel made of a hollowed cactus-stem, so heavy he could barely carry it, containing a thick, sweetish fermented juice which Arrheeharr scooped into bowls of the same material and diluted with fresh water before ceremoniously offering it to the guests. Creohan and Chalyth sipped theirs cautiously, finding it not unpleasant; hot and thirsty from her work at the fire, Madal gulped hers

down, nodded approval, and marched over to com-
mandeer a scoop of it with which to baste the meat.

Shortly the food was done, and they gathered around
the fire to begin their feast, the brothers on their
haunches, the guests on level rocks covered with skins.
The fare was not precisely to the latter's taste; still, they
were so hungry and Madal had made the meat so
appetising, they did not let nicety of manner hinder
them but tore with their teeth at the gobbets they were
given and returned for more. Curious stares fell on
Madal as the "brothers" tasted theirs, and Arrheeharr
declared he had never known meat so good. Hoo,
licking his fingers, studied Madal with interest, but said
nothing.

When they had all eaten their fill, Arrheeharr leaned
back with a loud burp of contentment. "Now we
should dance!" he exclaimed.

"Oh, it's too soon to dance," another complained.
"Let the food settle first."

"Very well then," Arrheeharr acceded. "But at least
we ought to sing. Hoo, you're the one with the memory—let our guests hear a ballad or two."

"As you wish," the dark man consented, and forth-
with launched out into a lengthy song, delivered in a
resonant baritone voice. The words were much inter-
spersed with what Creohan judged to be calls of the
meat-creatures, whose significance was lost on him, but
in general the theme was clear: some long while ago,
a mad beast had run amok through the herds, and a
herdsman of the time had stabbed it with a spear. Madal
reached for her harp and played a faint counterpoint
to the declamatory tune, which likewise caused exclama-
tions of wonder from the listeners.

When Hoo was done, they clapped and stamped and
shouted their approval; he himself, however, sat rock-

still until they fell silent, then addressed himself direct
to Creohan.

"You've heard one ballad—I think that should
suffice. Not all the world can be so concerned with
raising herds of meat as we are here in this valley."

Before Creohan could reply, two of the brothers got
up and began the shambling dance around the fire
which Arrheeharr had called for earlier, and all thought
of further singing was forgotten. The steps were like the
lumbering gait of the meat-creatures, and at first the
only accompaniment was the dancers' own cries, re-
sembling the meat-creatures' laughter, which brought
the beasts themselves curious to the edge of the circle
of firelight where they watched in silence. Shortly, however, the liquor having dulled the pain of her feet,
Madal began to evoke a wild skirling melody from her
harp which matched the irregular rhythm of the dance,
and within minutes it had become a crazy rout in which
everyone but Creohan and Chalyth appeared to have
joined.

Or not quite everyone.

A voice spoke out of shadow behind Creohan,
subtly pitched so that it could be heard clearly despite
the shouting of the dancers and the ringing of the harp.

"I do not detect in you the air of satisfaction which
ought to attach to the successful completion of a
hazardous mission, or the attendant relief at being able
to return home."

Creohan twisted where he sat, and found Hoo gazing
at him.

"Why—ah . . ." He fumbled for words. The dark
man's challenge had taken him aback; it was phrased
with such delicate indirection that he was afraid to
contradict it outright, for fear the deceit should be
apparent. He compromised on a half-truth: "Why, it's
true that our journey is not over, but it's no less true

that your meat has come faithfully and in sufficient numbers since I can remember and probably for long before I was born."

The dark man's mouth shaped a fleeting smile. "Oh, I'm not accusing you of lying to us. I doubt if you even misled Arrheeharr—at least not deliberately. And certainly it's a relief to know that there are people far away who have benefited from what we've done. For all we knew, we might have been acting out a meaningless ritual, alone on the surface of a devastated globe."

Creohan stared at him for a moment. Then he glanced sidelong at Chalyth and found that she was rapt in watching the dancers; he was able to draw away unnoticed and address Hoo privily in a lowered voice.

"For someone whose life has been bounded by the walls of this valley, friend, you strike me as strangely well-informed about the world!"

"Perhaps the last of our family to be so," Hoo muttered. "Unless the boy who's slumbering in the cave takes after me, since he's a son of mine . . . That's for the future, though. See you now: this is the way of it." He leaned confidentially close.

"I carry in me the seed of discontent, and it makes me much afraid for these my kin. You heard me sing that story-song which was made by my father's father's father's father. Well, that's the load I bear. I know others, many others, which I seldom sing, because they tell of a time when men and women from the cities we serviced came here often, to praise us and bring us the news. My brothers hardly understand anything in those songs, apart from the mention of people like ourselves, but I've spent long days thinking them over, all my life since I was first taught to sing them, and from that source I've drawn what knowledge I can claim to have, such as that the world is round, and circles the sun, and has on it oceans and cities, which

I've never seen. And what I feel is this." His face drew into a scowl and his hands sought a grip on the empty air.

"I feel a kind of curse is laid on us! Why are we happy here, tending our beasts and never going further than the brow of the valley? Other men explored the world, sailed the sea, levelled mountains, and that spirit is in me—somewhere!" He thumped his chest with a bunched fist. "It must mean something, that our visitors are separated now by generations when formerly they came in hordes, and every year! I think in short that our lives are going to waste, performing empty tasks for the benefit of distant unknowns who have never given us a thought of gratitude. Tell me honestly, stranger Creohan: before you encountered Arrheeharr, did you even suspect that we existed?"

Sickly Creohan confessed that he had not.

"So what's the purpose of your journey, then?" Hoo said. "Let Arrheeharr and the rest delude themselves— it's a harmless pat on the back for them. But I'm of different stuff. I want the facts."

Creohan swallowed hard. "A star's approaching Earth," he said at length. "That one, the very blue one, overhead. It will be drawn to the sun and its heat as it passes will sear our planet clean as an unskinned piece of meat would be singed clean of hair over the fire. And we are hoping to . . . No, I don't know what we hope to do!"

"I see," said Hoo. "Well, let me tell you this. To lose the world which has played such a scurvy trick on me and my family will not cause me to mourn! If I could draw down that star you speak of to burn the earth up tomorrow, I'd do it. And I'd laugh!"

He spat very deliberately into the fire, and rose and disappeared, leaving Creohan to brood alone on his dismal thoughts.

"Oh my life!" said Chalyth faintly; she seemed to have heard nothing of the words which had passed so close to her. "Creohan, look!"

She flung up a trembling arm, and Creohan saw that at the edge of the firelight the meat-creatures had aped the antics of the dancers, and were likewise shambling through a rhythmic pattern that kept time to Madal's music.

Astonished, Creohan uttered an exclamation, and Chalyth said passionately, "I feel as if I have eaten my brother!"

She leapt to her feet, face pale, and staggered into the darkness. Shortly, Creohan heard the sound of her laden stomach giving back her meal in expiation.

XII

AT LAST THE dancers grew weary; they began to drop out of the ring and go into the cave. Madal alone remained where she had been, the wild beat of her harping slowing into a gentle, nostalgic tune which made Creohan think of the remorseless passage of the ages. He also rose and felt his way into the cave. When he came to Chalyth lying on a heap of skins and sobbing very quietly, he lay down beside her, and sleep overcame them both.

In the dawn, they were roused by the others going about their business. They seemed tired, and yet there was a repressed merriment in their manner which made them now and then chuckle aloud, as though fresh heart had been given them by the news that their work was indeed of service to others. Creohan, blinking in the daylight as he left the cave, found Hoo's eyes on him, inscrutable, and could not meet that dark and level gaze.

The little boy, Hoo's son, led him and Chalyth around the rock to the place where the clear spring supplying them with water welled forth; the pool into which it spilled was divided with a dam, to separate a washing-place from a drinking-place. Chalyth, with a sigh of pure pleasure, stripped off her clothes and plunged in, but the water was icy, and Creohan contented himself with rinsing his head, hands and feet.

Returning to the cave he encountered Madal, hobbling forth on tender feet to which one of the herdsmen had applied cooling poultices of bruised leaves and grease, one hand toying with something hidden in her bosom. Nearby, Arrheeharr was engaged in burying the bones from last night's feast in a shallow pit, and when he saw Creohan he came to put a brawny arm around his shoulders.

"Never can I remember when we were so happy!" he declared. "It is wonderful to have you here. You must stay long with us, so that you can tell the folk of your city all about us when you go back."

"Ah—we cannot stay," Creohan said huskily, and as Arrheeharr's face fell, added, "No, I'm afraid we must continue to another city beyond here. But you've been so generous and made us feel so welcome that if we can pass this way again, we definitely will."

Tending the embers of the fire, banking them with ash to keep in their heat while they were unattended during the day, Hoo caught the words and stared at Creohan again. It was impossible to deduce his morning mood, but recalling the angry frustration he had voiced last night Creohan was not inclined to talk much with him today.

"So when must you depart?" said Arrheeharr.

"This morning, I suppose."

"No, that you can't! Haven't you seen how your friend's feet are cut and blistered? It would be torture to make her walk further than from here to the hearth."

That seemed true enough; true or not, though, it was a source of dismay to Creohan and Chalyth, for always they felt a sense of irrational urgency, as though every moment counted no matter how far off was the threatening star.

Then Madal spoke up. "There's no need to delay for my sake, Creohan. This is as far as I shall go."

"What?" said all her hearers in the same breath.

"I've made up my mind. Of all the people I have ever known, these are the only ones who live their lives for the sake of others, not themselves, and lying awake through the past slow hours of darkness I've seen that impulse clearly in myself. That was why I was so furious with Vence. I'd tried to live for his sake, and all I'd been able to give him was no more than what he could take from—from . . ." Words failed her, and she shook her golden head, eyes downcast.

"Look!" she went on after a pause, and drew out what she had in her bosom. Creohan saw that it was one of the yellow flowers from the wall of her house, its petals now withered, but the seedcase in their centre ripe and hard.

"There are five seeds in this pod," Madal said. "From each seed, I guess, will grow such another home as mine, so I shall plant them here around the rock from the sky. I could not ask to join these people unless I brought a gift to make up for the intrusion, and as you rightly told me, I've never had anything in the world more precious than my home. Not even Vence. Oh my life—not even beloved Vence!"

Her voice broke, and Arrheeharr, despite seeming to have understood little of what she was saying, made haste to comfort her.

"But if we— Well, so be it," Creohan yielded. "Chalyth and I can go ahead alone."

"No." Hoo spoke up, letting fall the shovel with which he was banking the fire, and advanced towards them. "I will go with you from here."

"What?" Arrheeharr demanded in bewilderment.

"Why not? It isn't right that of all the cities to which we send meat only one should think of thanking us. You will have an extra pair of hands here now, with many new skills. I can be spared to go to some other city and ask why they have never given us a thought."

"But then who will make the new ballad telling of the great feast last night?" Arrheeharr said piteously. "Who will teach the boy to sing the old ones, too?"

"The time for living on old songs is past," said Hoo. "Well, Creohan?"

Relieved above measure that Hoo had not deprived his "brothers" of their simple happiness by telling the truth about his mission, Creohan expressed the view that it was a fine idea, though privily wondering whether even Hoo's exceptional personality would enable him to break free of the ancient habits that had kept his forefathers isolated in this bowl-shaped valley for so many generations, and Chalyth, on coming back from her bathe in the spring as fresh and beautiful as a newly opened flower, raised no objection.

"Then we shall set forth with the meat today," said Hoo decidedly, and Arrheeharr let out a volley of protests.

"How can we spare three trained steeds? We have only ten all told, and it takes months to break another in!"

"You plan to waste Madal's talents on merely herding meat?" Hoo countered. "When you tasted the delicious cooking last night—when you've just heard her speak of raising houses for us such as the old songs tell of in the distant cities? Yes, three steeds can certainly be spared; that leaves one for each, and the boy won't be riding alone before another can be broken, will he?"

Brooking no further discussion, he threw back his

head and yelled three times in a giant voice. At once three of the grazing meat-creatures ceased their feeding and came towards the cave.

"There!" said Hoo. "Now, you two strangers, we can spend the time before the day's meat is due to be dispatched in teaching you how to ride."

"Too fast," Arrheeharr said. "Far too fast! Things should change slowly if they're to change at all, that's my feeling."

"Go then and fetch the others, and talk it out," Hoo said with thinly veiled contempt, and Arrheeharr accepted the idea as brilliant, departing at a run and shouting.

"Have no fear," Hoo muttered. "Of all the eight of us, I'm the only one who can play tricks with words. You'll have agreement for my plan in half an hour, and I take it you'd rather ride than walk the next stage of your trip?"

"Why—why, certainly," Chalyth said. "But how can you so lightly abandon your home and your family? Most of all, how can you leave your son?"

Hoo's face grew instantly sad. "Better to go than stay," he said. "This I have never told to anyone, for there was no one who could have understood, but . . . Well, from the songs of yore I know it is not good to breed and breed within a little group like ours. True, he's my son, that boy. But he is not like me. We know about the breeding of animals; we know, in fact, of almost nothing else. When it was discovered that the boy could not memorize the songs I learned when I could barely talk, would it not be a sorry blow to all my kin? Better, surely, that they should blame my departure than the subtle poison undermining our heredity!"

"You mean he's . . . ?" Creohan could not complete the question.

"A dullard," Hoo said curtly. "Less bright than Arrheeharr."

A sense of great sorrow overcame them, and they sat in silence.

Exactly as he had predicted, Hoo secured the agreement of all his "brothers" within a few minutes of starting to argue with them, though afterwards Creohan could not have defined the reason for this except to say that perhaps they were tempted by the prospect of more visitors and more excuses to hold feasts like the one last night. Whatever the grounds for their decision, though, they were pleased enough to spare time from their regular herding duties and instruct the novices in the art of riding the amazingly tractable and gentle meat-creatures.

Towards the end of the day, therefore, the three of them mounted and urged their steeds to join the herds selected to be put on the trail this day.

"To which city are we bound?" Creohan demanded, and Hoo shrugged.

"We may as well take any road except the one you came by. We have nothing to guide us except guess-work."

They turned and waved farewell to the herdsfolk, among whom stood Madal, very small and fragile compared to the huskiness of her new "brothers".

"I hope," said Chalyth sincerely, "she has made a wise choice."

"As wise as ours," Creohan said with conscious irony, and spurred his steed into the wake of Hoo's.

XIII

THIS STAGE OF their journey led through country different from before, much barer than the plain of yellow grass or the site of the city sown with puffballs. Here, low scrub with leaves of red, purple and deep seagreen clung to hillsides framing a narrow valley with a gentle downward slope, but the greater part of the ground was gravelly or at most fledged with a squelchy moss. Despite the jolts he received as his mount bounded along and the oppressive animal smell its coat exuded, Creohan could almost have enjoyed the ride but for one thing: the meat seemed so delighted to be on its way to death that manic laughter made talking, and very nearly thinking, impossible.

After a while, however, as the sun declined, it became necessary to ignore even that, and try to sleep, for on their final march the herds never stopped regardless of night or day.

At intervals Hoo jockeyed his steed close to the others' and passed them sips of cactus-liquor and hunks of cold meat which he had brought, and they could exchange a few brief remarks. Creohan was surprised how hungry he could become without exerting himself, and ate with a will, but Chalyth had to sweat out a fight between appetite and prejudice before she could make herself accept any of the food.

"Do you mistakenly think these creatures are like men?" Hoo asked, the second time she refused his offering. "In that event you're wrong. Remember, I've lived all my life among them; I've watched them from cubs to grown beasts. Never once have I seen them act as a man may do—without example, of his own free will. They do not speak among themselves and they have never created anything. They can only ape the doings of a man. And, I think, if they had any other creature to imitate, they'd as cheerfully copy it."

Slightly reassured, the third time Chalyth was able to eat.

The air grew warmer as they descended. Apparently unhindered by their burdens, their steeds kept pace with the leaders of the herd and tirelessly strode onwards. At last they came to a river that flowed along the lowest level of the valley, and Hoo glanced at the sky which was now darkening again.

"Meat should arrive in the city during the night," he said. "We cannot have more than another few hours' travel before us."

Splashing and leaping among the pools that fringed the slow-flowing stream, the meat jolted them and rubbed sores on their arms and legs; their muscles grew cramped with the extra effort now needed to cling on. Grimly they obliterated the pain from their minds, seeing that Hoo did not complain, and when the night advanced they were relieved to notice that the laughter of the herd-leaders was quietening.

"This must be near our destination," Creohan called, guiding his steed closer to those of his companions as he had been taught. "Yes, look!" He flung up his arm and pointed to where a host of lights circled in the sky. "Where lights gather, surely there must be a city."

But Hoo paid little attention. "I like this not at all," he muttered. "Can you not tell that the animals are nervous? Something is frightening them." He sniffed, shook his head as if unable to unriddle the information the air bore to his nose, and spurred his mount into a lumbering trot with which the others had difficulty in keeping up.

Shortly, though, there could be no doubt of what had so disturbed him. They detected the stink of a vast putrefaction, that loaded the clean night breeze with suggestions of all-embracing decay.

"Do you not hear something also?" Hoo demanded. "Far off, laughter like the meat's—but faint and dispirited!"

Now they emerged on to a table of rock overlooking the city, and hoped to see before entering it what had gone wrong, but the wheeling lights flew below them as well as above, and dazzled their attempts to peer downward. They had to contain themselves in patience as their steeds clambered down a winding track broad enough for only one at a time, with the stink growing fiercer after every yard of their progress.

"What are those brightly shining things that flap?" Hoo asked, and Creohan whistled one down to show him, at a point where the creatures were almost beating about their heads. Another moment passed, and they could see.

Ahead, the road was like a charnel-house. On the edge of the city nearest to them, herds of meat milled about pointlessly, seeming weak and on the point of collapse. They blocked the path of the new arrivals, and not all Hoo's urgings could thread them a course through the throng.

"Why have they stopped?" Chalyth cried. "I understood that meat went to a certain prescribed place, and there died of its own accord!"

"So it should be," Hoo grunted. "Clearly, the place appointed in this city cannot be reached. Dismount," he added, assuming command naturally, and they gratefully complied, rubbing their stiff limbs. But he did not mean to rest. He strode forward, and they perforce followed him, until they stood among corpses.

Dead meat lay tumbled about them, on the ground, in the branches of outlying houses that had run riot and developed into unbelievable tangles, anywhere. And death had not come kindly to the creatures, either; far from the cactus which had been their lifelong food, they had simply starved. The nearest carcases were fresh—indeed, some which seemed to be past hope still moved, writhing—but those beyond were crawling with the worms of decay, and in the heart of the city, to which the travellers penetrated with difficulty, there were clean white skeletons.

"So this is why one city, at least, did not send to thank us for our work!" said Hoo in a voice of tremendous anger, and while Chalyth and Creohan stood dazed by horror, he gave way to his frustrated feelings and ran in among the bones, smashing them with kick after kick.

All at once his temper subsided, and he returned soberly to where they waited, carrying something round and white on which the flying lights played fantastically. Since the city was decayed, there was no order or grouping of colour in the sky, just the mad whirling of a crazy rainbow.

"That—" said Chalyth, and swallowed. "That's a skull."

"It is indeed," Hoo agreed, and Creohan stared at it.

"I didn't know you sent out meat when it was as young and small as that," he began. Hoo cut him short.

"We don't!" He set the grinning bone on his shoulder, so that for an instant they thought they saw Death looking at them, and then Creohan realised.

"It's a man's," he said sickly. "So they are dead, the people of this city . . ."

The vista of desolation spread around him filled his mind with horrible imaginings. Perhaps their journey might after all be futile; perhaps they would have found the same whichever trail they followed from the valley of the meat, and his own city might be the last inhabited in all the world.

Chalyth gave a little cry and hid her face on his shoulder.

Then a noise came to them. Another. Sounds of movement, purposeful, distinct from the aimless shambling of the meat. Hoo seized the skull by the stump of its neckbone and brandished it for a club, looking around warily. Black shadows gathered among the heaped skeletons, and suddenly a man appeared, so boldly that even without the continuing noises which now came from every side they would have guessed he could not be alone.

He was small in stature, barely reaching Chalyth's elbow. His glossy brown body was protected with tough leather cuirass and leggings, and on his head was a round white half-helmet made from one of the meat-creatures' skulls. A broad axe rested lightly in his hands, and the reflected lights gleamed on its keen-honed blade.

He studied them for a while without saying anything. Seeming satisfied with the result of his inspection, he made a beckoning gesture, and a dozen others accoutred as he was sprang into view. Trying to keep

nervousness from his voice, Creohan said, "Who are
you? What do you want?"

"For da time been, you ull do," the little man replied. A mirthless grin accompanied the words. He
spoke with an accent unlike any Creohan had ever
heard—and with the contagion of dead languages introduced by the Historickers, his home city was full of
strange accents. But the man had spoken fluently; this
was presumably his native tongue.

"Com wid us," he added, and Hoo gave him a glare,
as though prepared to take on him and all his companions singlehanded.

"We would do better not to resist," Creohan coun-
selled. "Maybe these are the survivors of whatever
overwhelmed the rest of this city's people, and we may
learn—"

"*We* uh w'at overw'elmed dis people!" declared
the little man proudly. "Is well you doan resis'! Move,
move!"

Tiredly, the travellers complied.

Behind them the insane laughter of the meat grew
faint. The reek of rotting carcases was blown away
from this direction and they could breathe more freely.
But it was with a heavy heart that Creohan looked at
the wild-growing houses among which they passed and
read into the riot of vegetation the splendour which
must once have reigned here. The city must have been
twice the size of his own, as he had already guessed
from the much larger herd of meat sent forth to it. Yet
now it was a desolation.

Hoo kept his thoughts to himself, but it was plain
from the wide-eyed sadness on Chalyth's face that she
too was puzzling over the doom of this fine city.

They came into clearer roads, along which their captors escorted them at a near-run that strained their
weary muscles. Attempts to slow the pace resulted in

blows from the handles of the brown men's axes, and insults and jeers to do with the travellers' greater tallness. Creohan began to see a pattern in their captors' behaviour.

They reached a causeway, irregular now and patched with lichens, but which must once have been a handsome highway along the bank of the river. The river, indeed, was still there; logically, it would be the one the herd of meat had followed on the last stage of their journey. At the brink the party halted, and on glancing down Creohan saw a whole fleet of boats tied up to a cable stretched from bank to bank, bows to the sluggish stream. Men—all little, all brown of skin, all clad in leather armour—guarded them.

"Down," said the leader, and indicated a flight of steps slippery with moss that led to the muddy riverside. When they hesitated, his face twitched into a snarl, and with a broadside blow of his axe he struck Chalyth on the buttocks, so that she cried out, fell forwards, lost her footing, tumbled headlong to the stagnant mud.

Creohan looked at Hoo, and found that they had come to the same decision in the same instant. They had no stomach to be delayed on their quest by cocky little brown warriors. Forgetting their sores and their stiffness, they rounded on their nearest captors, Hoo taking the leader and Creohan another man, seized them by their arms and pitched them bodily to the water. Two splashes sounded as one. The guards on the boats jumped up with shouts of alarm.

How light and fragile these little men were, thought Creohan. But their axes were not. One whistled past his head as he dodged aside. The weight of the blade took the weapon to the ground before its wielder could recover. Creohan seized his chance and sent a second victim after his first. And another and another, while Hoo did the same.

"Did these runts claim to have overwhelmed this city?" Hoo said scornfully. "They're too weak to drag their own shadows after them! I'd like to see one of them try to wrestle with a rogue meat-creature, as I've had to do."

The causeway was clear but for themselves. Splashing from the water informed them that the little men were swimming to the safety of their boats. Creohan possessed himself of an axe dropped by one of them in his involuntary and quite literal flight from the scene, and started down the steps to see to Chalyth.

He exclaimed anxiously when he reached her. She had sunk to her knees in the marshy wetness of the bank, and her futile struggles were only sinking her ever deeper. A rusty metal ring was set in the wall of the causeway near at hand, and he grasped it while stretching out his other arm towards her. It was no use—the distance was too great.

"Let me!" said Hoo, and Creohan gave place; the other's span was longer than his. Chalyth tried vainly to come closer. The sucking mud was up over her thighs, and her face was pale with fright.

"So!" said Hoo, linking his fingers in hers. He tugged and hauled, and some slight progress was made, but not fast enough. There was activity out on the river, cries and the clang of metal, and they dare not delay until the brown warriors recovered from their first surprise. Creohan hunted for a foothold from which he could help Hoo, but wherever he trod he also began to sink in.

Without warning Hoo lost his grip on Chalyth's fingers, they being slippery with mud, and his feet splayed out from under him. Now were there two to be helped? No, luckily; he was recovering, taking care not to lose his footing again as he scrambled up. Creohan took his place at the ring, reached out to Chalyth—and saw, as he raised his eyes, that one of the boats had put over to the bank. Two brown men were hauling it along by the cross-river rope; two more sat on its thwarts with axes raised; and one sat in the stern, who voiced an incomprehensible command.

Fatalistically, Creohan wondered what it was like to die.

XIV

A MOMENT LATER he was stupefied to find that the words his mind had rejected were only disguised by speed of utterance and the brown man's unfamiliar accent. He understood them the second time very well, and they were addressed to him and had nothing at all to do with his being killed.

"Doan stan' dere like silly meat-beast, you! Catch rope an' t'read it t'rough dat ring!"

Rope? What rope? While Creohan was still gawping, Hoo reacted, accepting a cord which one of the men in the boat tossed to him, passing it through the ring, dropping a loop of it over Chalyth's shoulders. His and Creohan's combined strength brought her sliding across the mud to the foot of the steps, almost crying with relief.

But that was not the only trick with ropes the brown men knew. While they stood panting from the exertion, a second cord whizzed through the air, dropped over them, was pulled tight at precisely the correct moment, and they found themselves encircled at waist-height.

"Com 'ere!" said the man in the stern of the boat,

and the line was given an ungentle tug. On the slippery mudbank they could obviously be dragged if they didn't go voluntarily, and there was no reason why dragging should stop when they reached the actual water.

"All right," Creohan said, and they made their awkward way into the boat.

There was some grumble of complaint from the crew as they dripped mud over the bottom-boards, which was quickly silenced by the man in the stern. Creohan studied the latter with curiosity. Unlike his subordinates he wore a robe that hid his body from shoulders to feet. On his head was a woven cap dotted with glistering sequins, and laid out either side of him was a small arsenal which made Creohan rather glad they had agreed to come aboard unresisting, for it included not only a battleaxe such as the man ashore had carried, but two smaller throwing-axes, swords, knives and a quiver of wicked javelins. The members of his crew were similarly outfitted, though less lavishly; alongside every thwart in the boat there was a rack of weaponry.

"You uv cos' me t'irteen men," the man in the stern said before Creohan could speak, and Hoo spoke up defiantly.

"We only threw them in the river. They'll be no worse off than wet and sorry for themselves."

"Dey are not good to me no more," the man in the stern said. "Dey uv been beaten by a q'arter of deir number. See!" He gestured, and they turned to see a wet head bob up alongside the next boat out from shore. A guard on the boat raised and slammed down his axe, and the head went floating down the current. The body, spurting blood that looked black in the light from overhead, sank where it was.

Chalyth clutched Creohan's arm, biting back her horror at this casual expenditure of life. Apparently satisfied that he had made the desired impression on his captives, the man in the stern snapped another order, and the men at the bow hauled on the cross-river cable again, dragging the boat free of the mudbank where they had beached it and returning it to the middle of the stream.

"You uh not f'om dis city," the man went on, making it a plain statement.

"Ah—how did you know?" Creohan countered, struggling to overcome the revulsion which had affected him no less strongly than Chalyth.

"Och! Dis city's dead." The man spat over the side. "Like all da rest, dis city's been dead for long long time."

Chalyth gave a little gasp, and Hoo took a step forward which made the boat roll heavily. "All the rest are dead?" he echoed. *"All* of them?"

"Sure, all." Paradoxically, the man in the stern seemed sad at it. He made a large half-circle with his left arm in the direction of the nearer shore. "All over dere we roamed an' wandered, and we foun' always like dis. Again, again, again. Soon now my people com back from da city, and dey tell me w'at I a'ready know—dat dere is no one but da animals dat are like biggest men. An' you, only you not belong 'ere. W'ere you from, eh?"

"We are not from any city," Creohan lied, and to his surprise the man did not even question his assertion.

"Dat I know. If you came from a city, I ud uv conquered it. But dere are only dead cities now. Dis is da end for us, dat I do fear."

He was interrupted in his melancholy refrain by the arrival—hand over hand along the cable from the bank—of just such a cocky little man as had led the party they had been captured by. He hesitated with one foot on the bow on seeing the tall strangers, but a gesture from the man in the stern brought him nimbly down into the boat. There, he fell on his knees and reported, "Lord, we uv been t'rough da city. Dere is no one alive."

"Go!" said the man he had addressed as "lord", and he obeyed, to be followed by another and another and another—just as many, Creohan noticed, as there were boats beside this one moored on the river. And at the same time those boats, including their own, began to fill with little brown men who laid down their axes as they occupied the thwarts and took up broad paddles instead.

The travellers stood together at the lord's right, waiting for the string of reports to reach an end. Chalyth, in a whisper, complained to Creohan of the foulness of the mud on her body and asked if he thought it safe for her to go overside and rinse it off, but he warned that it might be taken for an attempted escape, and they had seen with what small compunction this lordling treated those who offended him. One, though, who seemed to be boatswain was displeased at the smears of mud he found on his return, and ordered a folding leather bucket to be dipped so they could cleanse off the worst of it.

At last one party alone had not filled its boat, and that, Creohan realised, must have been crewed by the men they so ignominiously defeated. The lord rose to his feet and shouted for it to be stove in and sunk, and with the movement a half-formed guess of Creohan's was confirmed.

The lord stood head and shoulders above any of his inferiors—but his long robe concealed tall wooden platforms strapped to his feet, which clumped betrayingly as he moved.

These little brown warriors, then, must be jealous of taller races, and it would be that jealousy which had driven them to lay waste cities such as this. Creohan saw no reason to doubt the truth of the boast which the cocky leader of the party they had first met had made: *"We* uh w'at overw'elmed dis people!"

And now there were no more populous cities for them to attack, they must be making a continual vain round of the scenes of past victories, in the hope of finding people once again—tall people whom they could humble and bring low.

"Sit!" instructed the lord, and they did so awkwardly. Chalyth and Creohan pressing close together on a thwart, for warmth against the chill of their soaking clothes, and Hoo on the bottom-boards, dark face brooding over the brown man who had so completely taken control of their destiny.

"W'at were you doing in da city?" the lord asked, and Creohan risked another outrageous claim, hoping that his analysis of the brown warriors' psychology was correct.

"You look for cities to conquer. We who are done with cities seek to conquer a star."

The statement made so bluntly filled the lord with sudden awe. His hand crept to the haft of one of the axes beside him, as though he felt he might need to protect himself from—from whatever he feared about people bigger than himself. Delighted, Creohan went on.

"You have searched up and down this coast—the one from which this river runs inland—and you have found only deserted cities. Is that not so? Why then do you go on searching?"

Pleased to find something the travellers did not know, the lord shrugged. "It is among our people dat before a lord can become a king he must prove self and sack a city of da biggest people. For ten, twelve genera-

tions we uv no king. My fader like me was only a lord.
For dere are no more cities to attack."

Creohan gave a thoughtful nod. It seemed that still
more of his guesses were being confirmed. In particular
he had established why the brown warriors had never
appeared at his own city. On their way here they had
crossed a ridge of hills; the valley of the meat was
somewhere near its highest point. Presumably those
hills spined an isthmus, and his home faced a different
ocean. That was as well—he hated to think what easy
pickings the warriors could find there.

"You must come from an island far out in the sea,"
he ventured, and the lord admitted as much.

The talk continued. Before the boat reached the
river's mouth he had confirmed all he wanted to know.
Far to the north and south the coastline stretched un-
broken. A short way inland lay the line of hills, which
these people had never crossed—they were tied too
closely to their boats to risk an overland voyage, so
they limited their range to the highest navigable stretch
of the rivers. In fact, he suspected that water-transport
so dominated their thinking they imagined no one
could live away from the reach of a boat, or at least
not in cities sizable enough to make this lord into a
king.

His tongue loosened, the lord began to boast of the
legendary exploits of his ancestors, as though he feared
to seem petty beside the travellers who went towards
a star. Creohan was only a little surprised to find that
his tales resembled stories he had heard from Historickers at home. The race of which these few boatloads of
marauders were the last remnant must once have made
a tremendous mark upon the world.

"And where do you head now?" Creohan demanded
at last when the sky was greying towards dawn and the

sound of surf on a beach had announced they were about to change from fresh water to salt.

"We go on," said the lord hopelessly. "Somew'ere—maybe even now—dere may remain a populated city."

Creohan rose to his feet, steadying himself against the rocking of the boat with a hand on Chalyth's shoulder. "We can guide you to a land where you have never been," he said solemnly. "We can show you the right course for a coast you have not explored!"

The lord, disliking to look *up* to Creohan, yet afraid to stand in his turn for fear he might lose his balance on his awkward stilt-soled shoes, shifted uneasily. "Den w'ere we shall go?" he demanded.

Creohan pointed skyward, to what had given him his sudden inspiration: a covey of lights fleeing homeward before the dawn from the deserted city they had left.

"Do you know all the places the lights go to?" he asked, and the lord shook his head.

Rapidly Creohan recounted how Hoo and Arrheeharr and their kinfolk kept the herds of meat, and how the beasts were daily dispatched along the various trails out of the valley. He had a near escape from exposing his earlier lie about not coming from a city, but covered himself in time by going on to the nub of his argument. Perhaps the lights too had a breeding-ground, he proposed, and flocks of them set out each night to cities on *both* sides of this great ocean. Then only let that breeding-ground be found, and the brown warriors might trail a flock bound in a new direction, with—who could say?—new cities at the end of the journey.

"You t'ink da lights com from da star you go to," the lord challenged. "You try to make use of me to carry you on da way!"

Creohan did not bother to try and correct that impression. He countered, "If you know you can gain nothing by roaming up and down this coast, you know you can lose nothing by searching elsewhere. True or false?"

A long mental struggle was clearly reflected on the lord's face: hatred of accepting even a suggestion from the bigger people he had captured being slowly overcome by the tempting prospect of becoming his race's first actual king in a dozen generations.

At last, with a glare so murderous it entirely contradicted the words it accompanied, he forced out, "True! As you propose, derefore, we'll track da lights."

XV

IT HAD BEEN an anxious moment for Creohan, wondering whether his suggestion would appeal enough to the lord's ambitions to allow him to compromise with his distrust of people larger than himself. Greed and frustration must have turned the scale; he could not hope that he and Hoo had gained any respect by overcoming thirteen warriors. And the anxiety was obviously, then, not over. They would have to be continually on guard against treachery. But at least they had been saved long and fruitless searching up and down the land they were now leaving.

But there was no chance to talk to his companions and find out if they agreed with what he was trying to do. The lord was keeping too wary an eye on them.

The boats rocked and staggered through the surf where the river encountered the sea. Dawn shone bright across a vast and featureless expanse of water. The lord cupped his hands around his mouth and gave orders that the fleet should follow the line the lights had taken, and no one questioned his decision.

Ignoring his passengers, the lord then lay down on

the after thwart, curling himself like a baby, and went to sleep. Cramped, uncomfortable, but willing, the three travellers did the same in the bottom of the boat.

When they awoke, they were out of sight of land, and they did not see a shore again for fourteen days.

The matter-of-factness with which these people undertook journeys beside which Glyre's vaunted trip to his deserted islands paled never ceased to amaze Creohan. They treated their boats as home; they slept, ate and drank without leaving their posts, their paddles across their knees. When there was need of food a group of men would be told to dive overboard and search the near waters, harpoons in hand. Seldom did they fail to return with great fishes, or clams, or polypods, or at the worst with clumps of juicy free-floating algae that—once the travellers had got over the qualms they felt at eating something which was still living when they got it to their mouths—drove hunger away swiftly.

On the second day, when the fleet had hove to for just such a fishing expedition, Chalyth went to join the swimmers, which Creohan thought was a risky venture in view of the lord's continuing mistrust of them. But she gained the admiration of all by returning with a fish bigger than two of the little men could have handled between them. Creohan watched with no little envy, for he felt lonely and lost in this waste of sea.

Worse yet, they had still had no chance to talk together openly, for they were confined to the space nearest the stern of the boat, at arm's length from the lord.

Under cover of the to-do which accompanied Chalyth's return with her prize, however, he seized his chance and exchanged a few words with Hoo. The dark man had kept quite silent since they came aboard, as though all purpose in life had been drained from him

by the memory of the dead city to which so many of
his ancestors had sweated to send useless food.

"Hoo!" Creohan whispered. "What think you of
these people?"

Hoo raised his bushy eyebrows and spat into the sea.

"Agreed. Yet may they not redeem their deeds of
savagery and violence if they convey us across the
ocean safely? They have already saved us much futile
time and trouble."

"Saved *you* from it," Hoo corrected dispassionately.
"I have no stomach for your vaunted mission to divert
a star. What I would do, were I free, is no more than
return home and tell my brothers how stupid we have
been all our lives. And one thing more! When we
do cross the ocean, and supposing we do find other
cities on the shore yonder, how will you be able to
quiet your conscience when these murderous little men
set about sacking them—hey?"

Creohan could not answer, and Hoo, giving him a
final glance of scorn, sank back into his sullen silence.

Shortly Chalyth came back on board, laughing and
merry, and having wrung out her long hair sat naked
on the gunwale to dry herself in the warm breeze.
"Creohan!" she called to him. "You must learn to
swim and come with us—it's wonderful down here! It's
so different from the shallow waters I have known
before."

Abruptly realising that she was failing to communi-
cate her excitement to him, she broke off and demanded
what was wrong, to make his expression so downcast.
Creohan briefly summarised the remarks Hoo had
made, but had no chance to hear her views before the
lord, who had been supervising the fishing, resumed his
place and shouted for the paddlers to re-commence
their rhythmic driving.

After that it became habitual for Chalyth to join the

fishers, and while the lord's scowl grew deeper his subordinates accepted her as a leader. It appeared to Creohan that only the lord himself suffered from true pathological jealousy of the taller captives, because they symbolised the ill chance which stood between him and the assumption of full kingship; his boat-captains imitated him, but the common warriors were willing enough to recognise talent where they found it, and Chalyth certainly possessed one which they admired. She could swim further away from the boats without tiring, dive deeper, and drag back more massive prey. Daily she tended to stay longer overside, straining the lord's patience to its utmost, until the morning came when he threatened to paddle away without her if she ever did the same again. Overtly contrite, she yet hid a grin as she turned away, and only Hoo and Creohan saw the look on her face.

Hoo, as ever, remained silent, but Creohan was worried. The charge Hoo had levelled against him was a well-founded one, and indeed if they discovered new cities on the far side of the ocean and the brown warriors sacked them it would be a terrible burden on their consciences. Over and over he cudgelled his brains for a solution which did not involve the risk of angering the lord and having them tossed overboard for their temerity. The best they could hope for was to stay alive and improvise when the moment came, and if Chalyth provoked an outburst of the lord's fury that indispensable precondition would be ruled out.

Daily the coveys of lights flitted overhead, confirming that the boats were maintaining the proper course, and time slipped away. The lord grew more and more tense, though he was at pains to hide the fact from his men, and Creohan caught many suspicious glances thrown at him. He was relieved beyond measure when at last his deductions were proved right; two or three hours past dawn on the fifteenth day a number of lights in their drab daytime garb were seen to strike downwards to a knob of an island looming on the very horizon.

Great excitement filled the boats; even Hoo roused from his apathy to look as they pulled in towards a rounded, greenery-fledged beach beyond which lights that must have numbered in the millions crowded and clustered, flying about, perching, sometimes even doing something Creohan had never realised they did before—squawking.

"You right dis far," said the lord from his seat in the stern. "I 'ope much you right *all* da way!"

"From here we only have to follow the line of flight of any lights that strike out across the sea in the opposite direction," Creohan pointed out, and was uncomfortably aware of Hoo's bitter eyes on him again.

They put in to a sheltered cove, and groups of armed warriors disappeared to scout the island, returning with two items of information: that the island was devoid of human beings, and that the lights smelled like good eating. Accordingly the boats were beached, a camp made, and orders given that the party was to remain until they had determined at what times and in what directions lights departed for the far coast.

Even the lord himself was so delighted by this proof that lands unknown to his people did in fact exist that surveillance of the travellers was greatly relaxed. Chalyth at once disappeared, and was seen thereafter at intervals bobbing among the rocks which studded the sea not far from the beach. Hoo did as Creohan had expected and walked moodily off by himself, leaving him nothing better to do with his time than to find out something about the way of life of the strange creatures which bred here.

And yet he learned little that he might not have

guessed from his home city. The lights nested on high ledges, from which families of young dived hesitantly and tried their as-yet unilluminated wings. They got their food by dropping hard-shelled molluscs from a height on to the rocks, or seized small fish unwary enough to break the surface. But the pattern of their adult behaviour—the reason for their precisely timed flights to cities which now had small use for their illumination—remained an enigma, testifying perhaps to Molichant's dictum about the skills of the past being lost forever. Certainly human intervention had brought about their instinctive actions; equally certainly the process had been set in train so long ago that scarcely even guesses could now be made as to the means.

Weary, he returned at the end of the day to the beach where the party had encamped, and accepted a portion of roasted light for his meal. As the scouts had suspected, their flesh was delicious. There was no sign of Chalyth, and he grew worried. He sat up long after he would willingly have been sleeping like his companions, until she stole up from the beach with a little of the phosphorescence of the waves still clinging to her hair.

"Where have you been?" Creohan demanded. "I've been worrying about you."

"I've been exploring, of course," Chalyth returned with an air of perfect casualness. "You know how much I'm always fascinated by the sea."

"At a time like this you can—" Creohan's voice, he realised, was too loud, and with a cautious glance around to see whether he had awakened any of the brown warriors, he dropped to a whisper.

"At a time like this you can indulge a hobby?" he reproved. "Chalyth, don't you understand that Hoo is absolutely right, and through my bumbling I may well be infecting the coast of some other mainland with the same plague which devastated so many cities we've left behind?"

The thought was actively preying on his mind now, and he had passed the whole period of waiting for Chalyth in reviewing what had been done at their first encounter with the little brown men, seeking and failing to find an alternative course of action which would have secured both their own survival and immunity from attack for the hypothetical cities they were bound for.

"What good does it do to talk about such matters?" Chalyth shrugged. "But for the chance of meeting these people we'd have spent months or years wandering about from place to place, finding nothing but the tokens of their nasty little conquests. For themselves, they're pleasant enough, but the ambition which drives their lord stinks in my nostrils."

"Of course!" Creohan agreed. "So how can you be unconcerned about the prospect of their falling on some miserable new victims the other side of the sea?"

"Perhaps because as I once said to you before, I feel Mother Earth is on our side, our cause being good."

That seemed like such an irrational attitude, Creohan was on the verge of exploding into anger. But Chalyth laid a warning finger across her lips and nodded her head sideways, and he saw that one of the camp guards was approaching, almost within earshot.

That was the last chance they had to talk together before, at daybreak, the boats were again launched into the surf on the trail of the lights which, as Creohan had predicted, regularly departed towards the further shore.

Only one thing seemed different about this leg of the journey, apart from his mood of depression having worsened. The sea was as wide, the rhythm of the paddlers only slightly less regular despite the staleness which overcame them progressively as day succeeded day, and the stoppages for fishing were as frequent. The thing that had changed was that, whenever he looked astern, he fancied he saw something in the water, following them, in shape like a blunt brown rock and in pace more than the equal of the boats. But no one reported anything peculiar on returning from a fishing expedition, and in the end he put it down as illusion caused by long staring into the bright clear water.

XVI

"WE ARE VERY near to land now," whispered Chalyth as she scrambled aboard after another plunge with the fishers on the twelfth day of their voyage's second stage and reclaimed her tattered clothes from the thwart.

"How do you know?" countered Creohan. "Are we in shallow water?"

"Not that I know of." Chalyth gathered a bunch of her dark hair and twisted the water out of it.

"Then what?" Creohan snapped. Ever since they left the island of the lights he had been trying to extract from her the reason for her apparently groundless optimism, or else to make her understand why he himself was so dismayed at the events he feared he had set in train. Maddeningly, she had prevaricated until he was half-convinced she simply did not appreciate the seriousness of loosing the brown warriors on an unsuspecting city. Yet she was by no means lacking in imagination. The whole problem amounted to a paradox which totally defeated him.

But before he could utter another word, Hoo spoke

up from near at hand. "You have little time left to still your conscience, then!" he said.

Chalyth gave him a look of wide-eyed innocence. "What's supposed to affect Creohan's conscience?" she inquired.

"You know very well!" snapped Hoo.

"Oh, I've already found a solution to *that*," Chalyth said, as though this instant realising what was on his mind, and wild hope blazed up in Creohan on hearing her claim. But—as so often during the voyage—the lord resumed his post a moment later and he had no chance to question her more closely.

All the rest of the day the mystery plagued him, until the sun set and they were once more overtaken by a covey of lights, which this time began to circle in their familiar wheeling swoops before they vanished over the horizon. As the night darkened so they themselves grew brighter.

The sight brought the lord to his feet, careless of his unstable balance. "Dere is a city!" he shouted. "Dere is da new city for us to attack!"

A cheer of delight went up from all the boats, and the paddlers began to put their backs into the work anew. The lord sat down again and studied his passengers quizzically. His fingers began to caress the haft of his favourite axe.

Creohan felt a pang of fear: suppose he did not even intend to give them the chance of reaching shore alive? Chalyth, however, appeared unworried, and even put a provocative question to the lord.

"Is it not dangerous to approach a strange shore at twilight? It may become too dark to call warning of sunken rocks."

"My men are too skilled to strike rocks even in darkness," said the lord carelessly. "Well, biggest people, I t'ink you uv paid price of t'irteen warriors you cost me. We uv no more need of you."

"So," said Hoo quietly, and rose to his feet. Creohan's heart sank; the lord's intention could be only too plainly read in his sneer of triumph. But Chalyth was as calm as before, and her only reaction was to nudge both her companions and whisper in a voice too low for the lord to hear.

"Now you're going to *have* to learn to swim!"

It would be a miracle if the lord let them go overboard in a state to swim, even if they could, Creohan felt. But an instant later, Chalyth had darted forward and snatched at one of the axes from the stern thwart—not to use, but to toss over the side, where it splashed noisily.

"Now!" she exclaimed, and herself took a tidy header into the sea.

The lord rose, shaking with fury; the paddlers shipped their blades and prepared to seize the remaining travellers—and the boat gave a sickening shudder as two of its boards were stove in amidships. A rush of water flooded around their feet, and the lord's rage gave way to panic.

Hoo was quicker to react than Creohan. He grabbed him bodily and tipped him over the side after Chalyth, following himself. Before the astonished brown men had got over their shock, Chalyth had swum up to them, her skin glimmering whitely under the surface.

Spluttering, and not a little frightened, for he was able to do little more than keep himself from sinking, Creohan nonetheless retained sufficient self-control to understand when she instructed them to slip out of their clothes for greater freedom of movement and follow her. Another of the boats was capsizing now, and apparently each in turn was being attacked by some unseen agency, which either holed it or spilled its occupants into the sea.

They had barely had time to digest that fantastic fact when a face loomed up ahead of them. It was a giant face, as broad across as a man's chest, and had a kind of humour about it. Creohan noticed at once that it was set on just such a brown, rock-like body as he had seen trailing the boats.

Chalyth swam up to the creature, gesturing and uttering words of praise; it wriggled as though from modesty, and Creohan almost expected to see it blush. She beckoned them, and under her guidance they took hold of the thing's muscular flippers, one on either side and she at the tail. As soon as they had a secure grasp, the animal began to swim by undulating its body, and despite the drag of its passengers it very rapidly left the little brown men behind.

The brilliance of the lights in the sky increased. The water became shallow enough to stand in, and at that point Chalyth directed them to let go. The moment they complied, the creature which had helped them swung in a tight circle and paused in front of her for a second. She patted the huge blunt head with affection, and then it was gone.

They stood chest-high in the shallows and looked up at the shore. There *was* a city here under the lights, though not such a city as Creohan was familiar with. Closer at hand a number of small boats were beached on a sandbar, and nets were stretched to dry on wooden poles. Everything betokened the recent presence of living people, and Creohan's long-downcast spirits rose abruptly.

"How did you work your miracle?" Hoo asked Chalyth. He too seemed to have recovered from his fit of dumb withdrawal.

"Once, long ago, his people were companions and

servants of human beings," the girl replied. "I had met many of his kind before—it was one such as he, Creohan, who brought me that golden helmet from the islands Glyre sailed to. Do you recall?"

"I do," said Creohan. It seemed as though a century had passed since she told him about that.

"He was so overjoyed when he met me, the first human in many generations to come among his folk and speak to them, that he readily agreed to swim after us and stay on guard. I told him that if I gave the signal by throwing a weapon overboard he was to butt in the boatsides with his snout."

"I wish I could have expressed our gratitude," Creohan said sincerely.

"He's well repaid, he said, for he will have a marvellous tale to tell when he comes home." Chalyth shaded her eyes and peered out to sea for a moment. "Let's not stand here, though. The little brown men will soon be following us. We can only have outpaced them by a little, and while they may not be speedy swimmers they will surely drive their muscles to the utmost to bring them ashore and save their lives. We must warn these people here—"

"They are coming to be warned," Hoo interrupted, and lifted a dripping arm.

Down towards the edge of the sea was walking a group of men and women with skins as yellow as old gold and liquid dark eyes. Some of them were clad in flowing blue or white gowns, but most wore short and occasionally ragged kirtles, with wood-soled sandals on their feet. They were of all ages; the tallest among them would overtop Creohan by half a head, but he was an exception. They chattered excitedly as they approached and Creohan realised with a sinking heart that he could not understand a word they were saying.

Nonetheless, he plodded forward to the beach, reflecting on what a sight they must look: all naked, he and Hoo shaggy of hair and beard—but clean, at least, after their involuntary bath.

One who seemed to be a leader among the yellow folk looked the newcomers up and down thoughtfully, and then addressed them in the strange musical tongue they had already heard. He had no weapons, nor did any of his company, and Creohan worried once more about their ability to deal with the brown warriors.

He said at length, "Do any of you speak our tongue?"

A man and woman dressed identically in blue gowns answered him together, speaking with a far better accent than the brown warriors. "Yes, some of us do!"

"Then take warning! Though they come swimming, instead of in their boats as they had hoped, there is a gang of cruel brown marauders approaching from the sea!"

"Little men?" said the blue-gowned woman, and on his nod, to their enormous surprise, gave a cheerful laugh. The man turned to interpret to the others, while she continued to Creohan.

"My name is Liang-liang, and I am a student of history. I know that many times in the past small brown men have come out of the east thinking to prey on us, but we have never had much trouble in driving them away. This time, thanks to the warning you've brought, it should be simpler than ever."

"The brown people have been here before?" Creohan demanded in surprise. "Why, they always denied even suspecting that there were inhabited lands this side of the ocean!"

"Quite possibly the present party do not know." Liang-liang shrugged. "They are afflicted with vanity as vast as their bodies are small, and since we each time drove them off with no difficulty they doubtless invented comforting lies and forgot their humiliating encounter with us. It has been three generations, certainly, since they last ventured to this coast."

Creohan's shoulders slumped as he thought of the days of mental agony he had undergone, pointlessly. Liang-liang made a sympathetic sound.

"We would not wish to seem unappreciative of the tribulations you've undergone to bring us this warning," she said. "Come with us to the city, and we shall feed you and clothe you and let you rest a while."

The group was breaking up; young men and women in kirtles were departing at a run along the beach, and the leader, who seemed to have been amused to hear Creohan's story as it was translated to him, chuckled quietly as he also turned to go. Liang-liang invited them to follow her.

Their path took them over soft smooth sand for a while, then onto dunes crowned with springy tough grass. Another hundred paces, and they were at the city, passing between houses unlike any that Chalyth and Creohan had ever seen, for they were plainly made by human hands and not grown from seed. They were simple and low-built and square, and around each of them was a plot of land where fruit-bearing plants grew in tidy straight rows. This was a community that differed radically from his own, Creohan realised, and wondered if here they might find knowledge which would enable them to do something—anything—to help avert the doom of Earth. At the least, he assured himself, these people would probably listen to him with sympathy.

"Creohan!" said Chalyth abruptly. "Look there!"

And he saw it with a pang of despair. Unmistakable under the shifting light from above, squat and bulky in the centre of a small open space, there reared up just such a House of History as those in the grove which

overlooked their own city. No other explanation occurred to him than that these people too must be obsessed with the vanished past, rather than concerned
about the as-yet unsettled future.

"Here too . . ." he said sickly, and did not have the
heart to complete his utterance.

XVII

THEY WERE TAKEN into one of the houses and given gowns of white soft fabric and woven sandals for their feet. Liang-liang herself combed out their hair and singed the beards of Hoo and Creohan to manageable length. Meantime, a young man brought small trays with tripod legs and set one before each of them; these carried cups of a nourishing and savoury broth, plump loaves stuffed with a purée of shellfish, and tart little red fruits coated in honey. Eating and drinking, they felt their spirits revive.

Their hosts did not as yet inquire into their connection with the brown warriors, apparently content to wait until the newcomers broached the subject themselves, but whether this was from politeness or lack of curiosity Creohan could not be sure.

In a while another young man came to the house and spoke in the native language; what he said appeared to amuse him, for he grinned broadly, and upon Liang-liang translating for their benefit the visitors realised why.

"If you are not too tired," she said, "you may care

to come back to the beach. My friend tells me that the first of the little brown men are swimming ashore, and the reception we have prepared for them should entertain you, I think."

"Tired I am," Chalyth said, rising from the cushions on which she had sat to eat her meal. "But the discomfiture of the little brown men is a sight I'd sorely hate to miss."

"Come then," Liang-liang invited, and they all three followed her.

She guided them to the shore by a different path, which ended on a rise capped with a dense clump of flowering shrubs, offering complete concealment. Parting the branches and peering out, she chuckled, then made room for the travellers to look also.

From here, they could survey the whole of the section of the beach where they themselves had arrived. A hundred paces distant, a group of the brown warriors had ranged themselves into a horseshoe shape, in all numbering twenty-odd. Creohan's guess was that these were the few who had managed to retain their weapons, which they held poised as they stared warily around.

Within the protection of this armed outer ring, others who had been overcome by exhaustion during their long swim were coughing up water, stretching cramped muscles, giving one another massage. While they watched, two or three more warriors appeared on hands and knees in the shallows, and their comrades went to help them ashore. There were fewer lights here than had been the case before, and Creohan's whispered question to Liang-liang confirmed that, as he had suspected, the creatures were being deliberately driven away.

"The menace of things half-perceived in twilight is the key to our plan," Liang-liang added.

"What else does it consist in?" Creohan asked.

"Out of sight, as we are, among trees and bushes are half a hundred of our people. You will see in a moment what they are about—ah, already I smell the smoke!"

It wafted pungently to their nostrils, and a few seconds later reached the little brown men, who tensed suspiciously. Those being massaged left the middle of the ring and joined the outside group. Bit by bit, the whole nearer edge of the city was being obscured by a mass of smoke. Abruptly a figure appeared within it, five times the height of a man, with a crested helmet on his head and a huge curved sword upraised.

Heartbeats later, another like him took form within the smoke-cloud, and another, and another, closing with awful slowness on the little brown men. As they drew near it could be seen that their eyes glowed hellish red and their mouths were full of immense fangs dripping greenish phosphorescence.

Hoo gave a muttered exclamation, alarmed at the monsters, but Liang-liang reassured him.

"They are only jointed dolls carried forward through the smoke," she whispered. "There are lanterns behind their eyes, and their teeth are smeared with a liquid made from fish-scales."

Creohan nodded. That was much what he had worked out for himself. But when a colossal booming voice rang around the beach directly afterwards, he could not repress a start of astonishment. It was as though a hundred people had spoken at once, crying, "I see you, little men!"

"That is our greatest singer, Tran-niong," Liang-liang informed him. "He's speaking through a long wooden tube to amplify his voice. Now see how the courage of these boastful fools wears thin!"

Indeed, some of them already had fallen on their knees or cast aside their weapons and fled incontinently towards the safety of darkness. One among them, whom

Creohan thought to be their lord, but at his true height now having lost his stilt-soled shoes in the sea, screamed with rage and belaboured them with fists and feet. That resource failing him, he snatched up a dropped sword and used it on the nearest he judged to be a coward. The man collapsed with a gash from shoulder to hip, howling, and that was the last straw. The most steadfast of the band could not bear to have their own lord attacking them, and took to their heels, some returning to the sea, others diving among the bushes where the natives easily made prisoners of them. Within minutes the lord was left alone on the beach, screaming defiance at the monstrous silhouettes in the smoke, which had now placed their sword-points on the ground and, leaning on the hilts, were studying him with a kind of amused tolerance.

"Fight!" screeched the little lord. "Fight, I say!"

But instead the vast figures looked at one another, gave simultaneous shrugs, and turned their backs to walk away. That was more than the lord could stand. By now foaming at the mouth with impotent rage, the lord reversed his sword, set its point beneath his chin, and flung himself forward to the sand.

There was a long moment of silence, as though the victors were dismayed at their own triumph, and lacked heart to utter cries of jubilation. At length Hoo said soberly, "Were I one of *them,* I should think this a land of devils!"

"They have seen nothing but their own fears, as if in a mirror," said Liang-liang. "Did they not roam abroad to attack peaceful strangers, they would not be ashamed of their small stature, for they are all alike among themselves. Such people are causelessly jealous, and it is easy to make them destroy themselves. But it is not pleasant. There are many among us who will sleep badly from now on."

Firmly, she turned her back on the spectacle of the body leaking blood, and gave them a courtly bow. "You're doubtless tired," she said. "Shall we return to your accommodation?"

They fell in behind her, and nothing more was said until they passed close by the same open place they had seen before, where stood the House of History. Then Creohan said, "Tell me, Liang-liang: is that not a House of History?"

"A Tree of History," Liang-liang countered. "Yes, a tool for students like myself who are concerned to search out the past history of our race. You've seen them elsewhere on your travels, I presume?"

"You use them for no other purpose than to gather knowledge?" Chalyth pressed her.

"Of course." Liang-liang sounded surprised. "What other purpose could they serve?"

"In our city—" Creohan began, and explained about the Historickers. Liang-liang was horrified at what he told her.

"But that's unworthy!" she exclaimed. "Our Trees are not freely open to anyone who wants to waste his life in dreaming! Would you have an—an artist lend his paints to any child who wanted to scribble on a wall? Those are the tools of our craft, and they're precious. Besides, they're dangerous in untrained hands, no less than a sharp knife. We have a great project, here in our city. We are analysing and setting into coherent sequence all the memories which our trees impart, attempting to trace the entire story of human endeavour. When the pattern is complete, we hope to grow a last and final Tree, so planned that one may enter by the door and pass slowly through, reviewing the whole grand panorama of human history."

"You have the skill to do that?" Creohan said wonderingly.

"We hope to acquire it, merely," Liang-liang admitted. "These Trees we have were not grown by us—they were brought here in the time of the Mending of Men, a thousand years ago, and our community has been at work on its project for not much more than three centuries. But we are daily gathering the necessary data. Already we have completely sifted and analysed as far back as the Lymarian Empire, fourteen thousand years ago."

"The Trees, though, have been in existence more than twice as long," said Creohan. He had learned that much from Molichant.

"I fear so," Liang-liang conceded. "But we shall come to the requisite knowledge some day, that's for sure. Now here we are!" She halted before the door of one of the typical low-built houses, and ushered them inside. "Your accommodation while you stay with us—I trust it's to your liking?"

Entering, Creohan found himself in a single large airy room, around the walls of which were disposed high piles of cushions in many bright colours. There were decorations hanging from the ceiling: scroll-paintings skilfully executed, jingling constructs of bells and metal wire, fresh flowers in tiny porcelain water-pots. A stream of warm water crossed one corner in a wide pipe of deep blue glass, knee-high and open at the top. From it wafted, with the steam, a delicate scent like ripe fruit. Chalyth ran straight over to that, dipped her hand in, and uttered loud approval, while Hoo—overcome by weariness—dropped plump on one of the stacks of cushions and leaned back limply.

Creohan, however, barely took in his surroundings, and Liang-liang inquired anxiously whether something was wrong. He roused himself with an effort.

"No, I was merely distracted! This place is beautiful.

I was thinking of the unlikelihood of your ever completing this grand project you've described to us."

"Why?" Liang-liang's voice was just perceptibly tinged with offence. "I assure you we do not lack the persistence it demands!"

"No, no, you misunderstand me." Creohan took a deep breath. "Had it occurred to you to wonder how we came to fall into the hands of the brown warriors, and voyage so far from our own home city?"

"Indeed. But we are not in the habit of demanding that our visitors should give an account of themselves before we extend our hospitality."

Another misunderstanding! But Creohan was too weary to sort it out. He merely summed up, in the baldest possible terms, the dreadful discovery which had led to his and Chalyth's departure on this random journey.

"This is a very serious matter," Liang-liang said, when she had heard him out. "And I apologise for mistaking the import of your earlier remarks. I must carry the news at once to Kiong-binu, our leader whom you met on the beach when you came ashore. And tomorrow, or as soon as it can be arranged, it must be discussed by the full assembly of the people! Leave it with me, then, and rest well, in the assurance that the matter is under urgent consideration."

Bowing, she withdrew. Creohan looked at his companions. "Well?" he said. "What do you think? These seem to be a sober and determined people—could they be the ones to turn aside disaster?"

"They have a rich store of knowledge to draw upon," Hoo said around a cavernous yawn. "More than that it's far too soon to say." He twisted sideways and lay down on the stacked cushions; almost at once he was asleep.

"Chalyth?" Creohan said, turning. But she had peeled off her gown and scrambled into the open pipe of water, luxuriating in the chance to rid her skin of the sea-salt crusting it. After reflection, Creohan decided that the most sensible course was to do the same, and clambered in to join her.

XVIII

HAVING BEEN AWOKEN early in the morning by the
same young man who had brought them food before,
this time with trays of identical-looking fist-sized rolls
each of which when broken revealed a different filling,
some sweet, some sour, some salty, but all good, they
were shortly after waited upon by Liang-liang again,
who gave every appearance of having slept little. Nonetheless, she was not impatient to disturb them, and
chatted lightly while they ate, telling something of the
origins of this community and incidentally demonstrat-
ing that the cult of the Historickers could not have
been unique where Creohan and Chalyth hailed from;
for, she said, when the ancestors of the present generation, who had been a hundred-member family of wandering bards and soothsayers, came to this place and
resolved to settle around the scattered Trees of History,
they found in several of them bleached bones, testifying
to the power which the alluring visions of a greater past
held over the minds of the ignorant and undisciplined.

Designedly or not, the gruesome reference encour-
aged them to end their meal while still some food re-

mained, and thereupon she informed them that at their earliest convenience they were invited to discuss their news with Kiong-binu.

Not wanting to seem discourteous to the chief of these folk who had generously taken them in, and eager to find out whether here indeed people might rise to the incredible challenge implied by the onrushing star, they set off at once, and as they walked to Kiong-binu's home Creohan plied Liang-liang with questions regarding the nature of society here. He had noticed, for instance, that roughly half the people wore long gowns, some blue and some white, while the rest wore the short kirtle and of the latter many were torn or soiled.

"The gowns," Liang-liang explained, "are a badge of involvement with the grand project I told you about last night. The blue indicates that the wearer is trained to enter the Tree of History and there absorb the memories elicited from the brain by the subtle neural stimuli—but I don't need to explain that, since you come from a place where Trees of History grow, even if they are put to the wrong purpose. And the white gowns show who is involved with the analysis of this mass of information, summarising it, recording precisely where and by whom it was garnered. As for the kirtles the rest of the people wear, why, they might go naked if they wished, but it is generally held that to dress is to express one's support for the project, regardless of whether the cloth is whole, or clean, or otherwise."

So inflexible a system was not entirely to Creohan's taste; he repressed his doubts, however. "Those who wear kirtles," he said. "What do they actually do?"

"They perform the services necessary to permit the students of the community to carry out their work," said Liang-liang. "Those services must be nearly the same in every part of the world: fetching and carrying, cooking, sanitation, gathering fruit and catching fish—

work of that order, too dull and repetitious to deserve the attention of an intellectual."

"So you have, as it were, honoured us undeservedly, by clothing us in these gowns?"

"Not undeservedly, I think. A traveller, too, after all, may be a gatherer and analyst of information, may he not? And in particular, after what you told me last night it became clear that you are a soothsayer, as our own ancestors were while they lived a nomadic existence. Now here we are at Kiong-binu's home; wait, please, while I announce you to him."

"A soothsayer!" Creohan burst out. "No, I—!"

But Liang-liang had already gone inside. Fretting, he stood with Hoo and Chalyth before the door of Kiong-binu's house, and examined it with some interest. It was large, obviously containing several rooms, and stretched between two Trees of History, as they called them here, whose topmost branches overshadowed it pleasantly. Its eaves were decorated with many strange symbols, a few of which Creohan recalled having seen at home, worn by Historickers, but most of which were wholly unknown to him and belonged perhaps to periods of the past which Historickers did not much favour.

When they were admitted, they were ushered into a large low hall at one end of which Kiong-binu sat on a high chair with padded arms. It was the only such they had seen, and they presumed that his great age or his office entitled him to it. They themselves were given low stools before him, and Liang-liang took another, and so did the two others present: a man of middle age introduced as Neng-idu, and a bright-eyed girl with a discontented face—Kiong-la, Kiong-binu's granddaughter.

The chief of the community greeted them with a number of formal inquiries regarding their health, their night's rest, their approval or otherwise of the hospitality they were receiving, all of which Liang-liang translated, and then proceeded to the important subject, from a standpoint which dismayed Creohan although Liang-liang's remark a short while before had partly prepared him.

"I understand you are a powerful soothsayer," said Kiong-binu, "and have predicted that a star will fall from the sky and prevent the completion of our work. Divination, to our regret, is an art almost lost among us—perhaps because scrying the past so deeply cannot coexist with prediction—but naturally this touches us very closely, and we wish to know more."

Creohan licked his lips, and glanced first at his companions, noting that they were as disappointed as he, then at the other natives. Neng-idu sat with a bland countenance as though the news of the world's imminent end was of no concern to him at all, but on Kiongla's face he thought he could discern attentive interest.

He said, "Well, it isn't exactly right to call me a soothsayer, and I don't ordinarily try and predict the future. I'll try and make it clear just what it is that's driven me to my present belief."

With that, there began the most frustrating day of his entire life, even worse than the time he had spent fretting at his own imagined bumbling aboard the boat of the little brown men, even worse than the sickening experience of trying to awaken interest in the citizens of his own homeland. For here—setting aside the culminating annoyance of having to wait after every sentence for Liang-liang's translation—there was the terrible, tantalising sensation that an unclosable gap existed between what he said and what his hearers, including Liang-liang, understood.

It was not that they were ignorant of the true nature

of the stars; many cultures whose achievement these people had examined had been well-grounded in astronomy, and though certain words like "telescope" were unfamiliar to Kiong-binu and needed to be explained at length, he was aware that the knowledge had been garnered even though he had never bothered to investigate the means employed. Nor was it that they lived for the present moment, either—no community centred on a project to evaluate the entire hundred-thousand-year span of history could be so temporally parochial. Above all, they professed to respect the ability of their ancestors to foresee the future, and maintained a deferential attitude to the visitors throughout, as being masters of knowledge out of time of equal merit with students of the past.

Yet there was no trace in their words or manner to suggest the same response as had overtaken Chalyth, Creohan and even Hoo: that sense of tragedy which had sent them on their quest. The entire tone of the discussion was as unemotional as if they had been talking about an event whose outcome had been fixed ten thousand years ago.

Kiong-la, perhaps more than the other three, appeared to feel the import of what he was saying, but she said almost nothing, and he deduced eventually from what few remarks he'd heard—in his own language, not having to be translated by Liang-liang—that she was here on sufferance, possibly because she had pleaded with her grandfather to be allowed to meet the strangers.

Noon passed; various foods were brought; the talk continued with maddening thoroughness, past remarks being searched over and over to ensure that the correct meaning had been assigned to certain words, that the reference Creohan made to "telescopes" and "stars" and "years" and "collision" agreed with what other cultures scattered over the past fourteen millennia had meant by corresponding terms in other tongues. More and more irritated, Creohan glanced at Kiong-la and was relieved to see her shake her head and pout her lips, as though to signal that she well appreciated how he must be feeling.

Hoo, however, found the slow progress of the discussion more than he could bear. At last he spoke up, his voice at a polite level but his face taut-muscled with the effort of controlling it.

"Please ask Kiong-binu," he said to Liang-liang, "whether he fully accepts that Creohan is telling the truth, and if so, whether he intends to do anything about it."

Liang-liang gave him a puzzled stare. *"Do anything?"* she echoed, as though the words were obscene. Instantly a great light dawned on Creohan, and he wished that he had never chanced across his terrible secret.

"Yes, do about it!" Chalyth chimed in.

"But I've told you," Liang-liang said with an air of infinite patience. "We are calling a meeting of the full assembly, and we shall consider it as thoroughly as we can."

"And nothing more?" Chalyth demanded.

"Why—ah . . ." Liang-liang seemed bewildered. "What else is possible?"

"We don't know," Hoo said. "But someone else among you may."

"That's to be seen," Liang-liang said, appearing relieved. "Yes, it's entirely within the bounds of conceivability that someone among us may have run across applicable information, and we shall be happy to share it with you. Let knowledge always be shared—that's a basic principle of our community."

Hoo, Chalyth and Creohan exchanged glances. "And

that's the maximum of your interest?" Creohan said at
length.

"You have shared knowledge with us; we shall share
knowledge with you, if we have it."

At this point Kiong-binu interposed what Creohan
took to be a request for translations, and there ensued
a short delay. When it was over, Chalyth—who had
been bursting with impatience—said, "And if there is
such knowledge, won't you act on it?"

Liang-liang looked shocked to the core of her being.
She drew back stiffly. "*Act* on it?" she echoed.

"Of course! If it turns out that something can be
done which—"

"Are you requiring us to *soil our hands* with labour?"

"Well, clearly, if—"

"Nothing's clear!" Liang-liang snapped. "I suspect
you're infringing the rights of a guest. First, I suspect
you're after a prejudgment of the full assembly's decision; second, I suspect you're asking us to do manual
labour; third, if the second point was mistaken, you're
asking for people to do manual labour on your behalf,
and we are a small community and cannot spare anyone for other people's tasks."

Stunned, Creohan said, "But it wouldn't be for our
sake! It's to save the planet Earth with everyone on it,
including you! Surely, if it turns out that somebody
does know a way in which the Earth could be saved,
Kiong-binu would direct that—"

"Enough!" Liang-liang snapped. "There is no sense
in continuing this discussion. What you are saying belonged, I always thought, to the barbarian past. Imagine Kiong-binu giving *orders* to students to dirty their
hands—it's obscene, that's what it is!"

She jumped to her feet, seething, and fired a rapid
volley of words at Kiong-binu and Neng-idu. Their
faces set like solid rock, and they too rose, giving each

a sketch for a frigid bow towards the visitors before marching out of the room. With a final scowl Liang-liang followed them, leaving only Kiong-la behind.

The air seemed to have turned to ice around Cre-ohan. He was unable to move for long seconds, a colossal despair pervading his mind. When he at last made to rise and head for the door, however, he realised that Kiong-la had not moved either, and that far from being angry she was smiling.

"Don't worry about them," she said. "My grand-father is a total conservative, and has never in his life looked further ahead than tomorrow's breakfast, so he surrounds himself with people of the same stamp. We're not all like that, though. I have a friend called Paro-mni, who is very ingenious in playing on the emotions of a full assembly of our people. I think a subject like this would give maximum scope for his talents. We'll see if I'm right. Meanwhile, as I said: don't worry!"

She gave a mischievous grin and walked away.

XIX

"I CAN'T MAKE head or tail of these people," Hoo muttered aggrievedly for the dozenth time, and Creohan sighed.

"I've told you my view! I think they've simply spent so many generations in unqualified dedication to the study of the past, they've lost sight of the platitude that there's a first time for everything. They didn't mind taking action to scare off the brown warriors, because that had already been done a number of times, but faced with the prospect of a situation without precedent they simply fold up mentally and pretend it'll go away. It must be costing them frightful effort to lay on this meeting today."

"Whatever the outcome," Chalyth said, "I don't think they'll be of any practical help."

"No, I'm afraid you're right. But, as Hoo said on the night of our arrival, they do have access to an incredible fund of information. Even if they decline to do anything themselves for fear of 'soiling their hands', they may put us on to someone else who's not so squeamish."

"That's a point!" Chalyth said, brightening. "I hadn't thought of that."

"Well, we'll find out soon enough," Hoo muttered. "Here comes Kiong-binu now."

They were on a high wooden platform at the centre of a small natural amphitheatre, a short distance inland from the centre of the city. Its sides were dotted with perhaps as many as two or three thousand people in the long white or blue gowns of the favoured "students", the younger of them seated directly on the springy grass which fledged the slopes, the older on stools or inflatable cushions, with awnings on cane frames to shield them from the sun. The non-students of the community were, as they had been informed, permitted to hear but not to speak, provided they were not on duty at their daily tasks, and about another thousand stood at the very rim of the amphitheatre in their short kirtles.

There was a pleasing simplicity and directness about the lives of these people, Creohan reflected. But he was mortally afraid that their culture was also rigid, and he had heard over and over from Molichant that in the end only one fate could be in store for an inflexible society: it would fragment, and someone would have painfully to put its pieces together in a new arrangement before anything fresh could succeed it.

Now Kiong-binu took his place at the centre front of the platform, according the travellers a frigid nod. With him had come Liang-liang and Neng-idu, and their manner was even more distant. Since the conclusion of their private meeting yesterday, Liang-liang had avoided them except to make sure they found their way to the place where they were staying and were furnished with food. They had hoped that Kiong-la might seek them out and introduce them to Paro-mni, the man she had spoken of as being potentially able to help them sway the assembly, but she had not come to call on them.

All three of them felt pessimistic about the outcome of this discussion. Searching the crowd with his eyes, Creohan tried to spot Kiong-la, but failed. She must be sitting too far away for him to recognise her among the relatively uniform faces of all these gold-skinned people.

The proceedings began with a long and detailed address by Kiong-binu, whose voice was not strong but did carry well; Creohan presumed that he had been accustomed to speaking in this amphitheatre for so long that he automatically timed each word to the natural resonance of the rocky bowl. He spoke, of course, in his own language, but Liang-liang had seated herself close to the travellers and interpreted for them, her voice emotionless. Creohan wondered whether she was giving an exact rendering, and decided that it would probably go against her people's nature to do otherwise.

Apart from the bias which he had no hope of correcting—the notion that anyone who made predictions must be a soothsayer like these people's ancestors—the summary Kiong-binu gave was a fair one. He descibed the travellers' arrival, continued by referring to the threatening star, and concluded by repeating Creohan's own view of the consequences of its near approach.

Following that, a number of speakers from the floor of the amphitheatre filled in details; these, Creohan gathered, were specialists in periods of history appropriate to the description of devices like telescopes and concepts like interstellar distances which might be foreign to some of the audience. It seemed all very calm and reasonable, and Creohan's hopes began to mount again.

There was an interlude for discussion among the

audience, which lasted the best part of an hour, and at
last Kiong-binu turned courteously to the travellers
and offered them the chance to speak before the con-
cluding formal arguments and the decision. Creohan
rose nervously, and scattered at strategic intervals
throughout the audience persons Liang-liang designated
as interpreters rose likewise, ready to translate for the
benefit of those who did not speak his language.

"When we set out," he said, "we had in mind no
more than to find someone who would share our dismay at the doom of Earth—fellow-mourners, if you
like. As we have travelled it has become clearer and
clearer to us that this in itself is pointless. It seems that
we should rather be seeking a course of action to prevent the catastrophe. Whether there has ever been a
time when petty humans possessed the skill and power
to interfere with the course of a star, we do not know,
but it seems to us that you who have delved more
thoroughly into history than anyone else ever has may
hold the key to such knowledge, if it exists."

He paused while the interpreters completed their
work, and before he could go on someone called, "He's
right! It must be done! May I speak, Kiong-binu?"

The old chief scowled. "It is not seemly to interrupt,
Paro-mni!"

Recognising the name with a pang of relief, Creohan
said hastily, "I'll gladly yield to him."

"Very well then," Kiong-binu sighed, and Paro-mni
rose. His eye guided to the right spot now, Creohan
was able to pick out Kiong-la sitting next to the new
speaker, a tall man as these people went, with a shock
of untidy dark hair which he kept having to brush away
from his eyes.

"Friends, we have tied our entire lives to a grand
project, the analysis of the whole of human history.
I put it to you that all our work will go for nothing if

this disaster takes place. Therefore we must digress for a while from our straightforward course. We must search out the necessary knowledge, apply it, and—"

A flood of protests burst out. Liang-liang expressionlessly translated a few of them: "We cannot leave our work to soil our hands with drudgery! We cannot condemn our children to be slaves!"

Creohan stared in bewilderment. Were these people quite insane?

"I would speak in answer to Paro-mni," said the benign-faced Neng-idu from the platform and on Kiongbinu's nod continued, "To the contrary, Paro-mni. It is my view that there is an inexorable force of fate at work here. In the two hundred and eighty-eight years which remain to us, we shall just be able to complete our project. The implication is that when the analysis of human achievement is over, so too will be the purpose of our species. We must not digress. We must complete our glorious task as we have always planned, and thereafter nothing will ever matter again."

Vigorous nods and cries of assent greeted his declaration, and Hoo gave an audible groan. Chalyth clutched Creohan's fingers so tightly, the grip was almost painful.

During this interruption, Paro-mni had remained standing. When the noise died down, he said, "Kiongbinu, I had not yielded the floor. May I continue?"

Kiong-binu gave him a grudging nod.

"I challenge Neng-idu's view! If there is one conclusion to be drawn from our study of history so far, it is that so-called 'inexorable fate' is the cause-and-effect working out of human weakness. I do not believe we are so weak we must resign ourselves to the knowledge that our children—whom so many of you decline to make into what you term 'slaves'—are to be burned alive! That would shame us before these three brave strangers, who may lack knowledge, who may lack power, but who most certainly do not lack determination!"

He jutted his chin aggressively and sat down, letting loose a storm of argument which Kiong-binu was as helpless to control as a bobbing cork to direct the waves which toss it about. It went on so long that Liang-liang gave up trying to interpret what was said, so long that people apparently grew weary of it, and at the psychologically correct moment a calm voice cut through the hubbub, that of Kiong-la.

"I propose a compromise," she said to her grandfather. "Will you hear it?"

"Yes, let us hear it," the old man said with a shrug.

"Clearly there is a divergence of opinion which cannot be resolved in a single meeting. I take it that this divergence represents two genuine strands of thought among us. Let us act accordingly. Let us who so wish furnish these strangers with the information they want, if it's to be found; let the rest, who do not wish to become involved, do as they choose."

There was an electric pause. Gradually people began to nod, and some rose to leave, satisfied. Kiong-binu, reluctantly, declared that to be the only solution and himself concluded the meeting.

Directly he and Neng-idu had left, Paro-mni and Kiong-la approached the platform and addressed the three travellers, the former quivering with suppressed rage.

"Well?" he shot at them. "What do you think of our fine proud community of scholars?"

Hoo answered promptly; he too had had difficulty containing himself. "If everyone on this planet were equally short-sighted, I'd say let them all fry—they aren't worth doing a hand's turn for. Do they think a star is to be turned aside with shadows, like the little brown savages?"

"I don't blame you," Paro-mni said. "No, I do not!"

"But at least we secured something from the meeting," Kiong-la said. "We put grandfather's nose out of joint—and that smug fool Neng-idu's. Did you ever hear such arrogance? Not even the Glorious Gerynts dared to offer their ideas as the unsurpassable climax of human endeavour!"

"But what exactly did we gain?" Chalyth inquired timidly. "I'm afraid I was so confused—"

"Why, this much," Paro-mni cut in. "You now have free access to all our Trees of History, with the help and guidance of such of our own students as feel the opposite to Neng-idu, and can search them for whatever information may suggest a course of action. Naturally, this is only the beginning, and we shall have to look elsewhere for people to carry out that action—here, we'll be lucky to muster a couple of dozen sympathisers."

Creohan recalled his own disastrous venture into a Tree, or House, of History, in his home city. Dismayed, he said, "We too are to make mental voyages into the past?"

Paro-mni shrugged. "We'll have to train you. It requires much discipline to comprehend the surging memories a Tree of History evokes. But we shall need all the help we can get, as I told you."

"Speaking of help," said Hoo, "*is* there indeed any group of people anywhere who could undertake the task before us if we find the means?"

"You've not run across any on your travels?" Kiong-la countered.

"If we had, would we be here?" Hoo said reasonably.

"No, I suppose not. Well, the answer's no—not on

this coast, anyway. Southward lies only a giant island where there are savage and fearful beasts. To the west, though, our hinterland is the continent where most of the great periods of human history have blossomed, and it is not impossible that somewhere there . . . Too soon to talk of that, though! Without sharing the revulsion of our fellow-citizens against working with their hands, I do feel it's pointless to consider recruiting forces for an impossible undertaking. Let's set to as quickly as we can to determine whether the job can be done. We've never before attempted to train adults to analyse memories from the Trees of History, but I imagine that with your dedication to your cause you'll find small difficulty."

"I hope you're right," Creohan sighed. "Well, then, the sooner we start the better."

XX

To Creohan's infinite relief, the Trees of History here were a completely different proposition from their cousins in his home city—perhaps, he reasoned, because of the different purpose they had been applied to over the preceding centuries. There were even maps available, detailed up to the epoch of the Lymarian Empire, giving sketchy highlights for ten millennia before that, showing in which Tree at which point in all its branching internal passageways persons of a given mental type would most readily respond to the subtle neural currents. Despite all the exercises and tests to which Paro-mni and Kiong-la subjected them beforehand, he was still apprehensive when he first actually ventured into a Tree; upon finding that he was not here overwhelmed by the confused tumult of memories, but could retain his own awareness throughout, he forgot his fears and took readily to the experience. He even began to feel some of the fascination which Molichant had tried and failed to explain to him. But the known urgency of their task struggled against and successfully held down the temptation to luxuriate in the welter of visions the Trees afforded him.

Chalyth, similarly, was entranced by the infinite corridors of past time opening up before her, but she had been a person of the present day all her life, and that immunised her against obsession, while Hoo's chief response seemed still to be tempered with bitterness, for he could never forget how his kinfolk had been tricked into a dead end of existence.

He did not suggest attempting to release them from it, though. He was too hardheaded to imagine that any of his family, except himself, could be happy away from the generations-old routine that occupied their days. The outcome of that problem must be left to the inevitable workings of time. Respecting the mental agony which the knowledge must be causing him, Creohan and Chalyth never spoke to him of his family, or of Madal, whose intervention into the static situation in the bowl-shaped valley might—just conceivably—have sown the seeds of their eventual escape.

Thus, after many long days of exercises and preparation, began the most crucial study of the past ever undertaken by human beings.

Before the Lymarian Empire, as they knew, had been the Glorious Gerynts, but they had concentrated on welding their people together into a single uniform horde; Creohan had unpleasant recollections of the effects of that.

Before them again were the Lucothids and the Pretascans, who had divided almost the entire planet between them and had trapped the heat-cycle of the atmosphere to power giant drifting cities which farmed the oceans; this age Chalyth identified with excitement as the era when the creatures she had grown friendly with in the sea first made the acquaintance of men, but they were not the people whose fallen cities had been visited by Glyre. Those were later decadents, for all his vaunting of their great accomplishments.

Before that were the Tymoletri, and the Gwams, and the Tridwelion, who had been like and yet unlike a thousand other cultures; before them again, the Minogovaristo. These were people who had drawn the clouds together as a back-drop for shadow-plays covering whole continents, but their domain, like their successors', stopped at the edge of space.

Before them the Dos had reigned, and the Glygly, and the Ngrotor; before them, the Chatrik, whose domain had *not* ended with the frontier of the air—but they had been content to plant huge forests of mutated lichens across the face of the now-vanished moon, which ultimately ran wild and digested all the satellite's substance into organic matter that was sprayed out and seeded into nowhere, leaving a mere mist of particles to testify to the former presence of a solid astral body. Likewise they had built pyramidal uninhabitable houses, or temples, on the arid soil of Mars, for a purpose comprehensible only to themselves. *They* could not have turned aside a star . . .

Half a year went by. Creohan, Hoo and Chalyth could scarcely reckon the passage of time any more, for they were now as skilled as Paro-mni and Kiong-la at skipping through memories that covered centuries, seizing one here, another there, and discarding all that was irrelevant. Waking to one age, slipping into sleep from the vision of another, made the present moment seem insignificant, and by now they were no longer so harsh in their judgment of these people who had declined to commit themselves to a present-day task as they had formerly been.

Before the Chatrik were the Pledowzi, whose main problem had been to contend with the depredations of a race of lizard-like people who had emerged from ruins sunk in a great ocean and struggled for the ownership of the land. The Pledowzi, being merciful, had spent five centuries adapting the harsh hot planet of Venus for these creatures' use; then they deported them thither by force. A possibility? All five of them studied that period for a week, and then admitted that the Pledowzi could not have swung aside a planet from its course, let alone a star.

So onwards into the deep, deep past, encountering the Kinkakans, the Dwyge, the Combara Comita, the Thnab—petty societies who left behind perhaps one folk-tale apiece and some houses which rotted. Then there were the Umftiti, whose homes grew like the ones to which Creohan was accustomed, and who handled plants with skills they themselves did not fully comprehend, as though a gene for sensitivity to vegetation had briefly cropped out of the planet-wide human pool, but never made the necessary connection with rational consciousness. So when the Umftiti passed away, the groves of their trees stood waiting until the period, twenty-nine thousand years later, of the Mending of Men, when the purpose such growths could be put to was rediscovered.

It was the Umftiti also who had first conceived the Trees of History, but they had been unable to control what they had invented, and their successors the Thnab had not understood any of it; so that too was left for twenty-nine thousand years.

Creohan wondered whether it was they whose city-site, now sown with those horrible transparent puff-balls, had been smashed by the meteorite which created the valley where Hoo's kinfolk herded their meat. But, of course, there would have been no survivors of such a catastrophe, and therefore that must remain a guess.

As the wave of humanity surged back and forth

across the planet, a pattern suggested itself: an age of machinery gave way to an age of working with living things, until the temptation to tamper with man himself grew too strong, whereupon the culture degenerated into violence and a return to machines. The sequence was not orderly; sometimes the collapse of a biological culture reverberated through two, three or more succedent ages. But the main pattern held good. The nearest approach to a combination of both trends had been achieved by the Lucothids and Pretascans, and they had advanced only a little way with the mastery of matter before they were seduced like so many before them into a single obsessive preference—and destroyed themselves.

Beginning to despair, the hunters skipped ever greater periods. There were gaps, too—real ones, when a continent might be unaccounted for. These were usually in ages when a culture was dying and chance weeded out its descendants one by one until none were left. Whatever the force was which evoked visions of bygone ages in contemporary human brains, it seemed to depend indispensably on the present-day survival of stock that led back to the desired epoch. Whole societies might thus have gone beyond recall.

Still, it was a consolation that what they were looking for must be found among a technically-inclined culture, and since these had in general spread over the entire Earth they were the least likely to have been lost.

Fifty thousand years in the past they chanced across the Muve, who had undertaken to divert the course of the planet Mercury in order to save their despotic ruler from an unfavourable astrological conjunction. That was more like it! Only the Muve had failed in their task, and the effort had so disheartened them that they collapsed in a disastrous war which altered the shape of mountains and caused many islands to sink from sight completely. Frustrated, the seekers pressed on.

The memories were growing dim now, overlaid by a multitude of resonances. Clearly, they were approaching the limit of variability the human race was capable of. An event detected as a tantalising glimpse might prove to have been reinforced by echoes from cultures a thousand, five thousand, twenty thousand years away, until it was impossible to extract a single uncontaminated group of facts. A few great cultures stood out brilliantly even yet: the Cursiles, the Lomril, the Slarf, all of whom had attempted to travel to the stars, and none of whom had truly succeeded.

A year went by, and the time came when Paro-mni said during their evening meal, at which it had become their custom to compare the information they had garnered during the day, "We are at an impasse! The density of data now might defeat the concerted efforts of our entire people—if they ever get so far! This is a problem we had not foreseen, this mixing of events millennia apart."

"Why should we have guessed at it?" put in Kiongla. "In three hundred years we have pushed our frontier of investigation barely beyond the Lymarian Empire. Now we're at the seventy and eighty thousand year mark."

"Granted. But now we're finding not one but several civilisations which may have held the key to the powers we need. Is it not maddening to discover they're wrapped in mist?"

"Why they, and no one after them?" demanded Hoo. "One might almost think there was once a—a breed of men, so to say, to whom the stars formed a challenge, and who have died out, leaving the rest of us content to live on a single world."

"It cannot have died out completely," said Creohan. "It is only your willingness to leave your lifetime home and come with us, writ large."

"One thing that does suggest itself to me," mused Kiong-la, "is that knowledge of the behaviour of inorganic matter has become progressively a less sought-after goal. The opposite trend, to an understanding of man himself, has been exemplified in our own community."

"But you cannot divorce the two," said Paro-mni firmly. "I have often suspected so, and the news of the threatening star proved it to me. What becomes of our grand attempt to comprehend mankind when there are no people left to appreciate it?"

"I scent defeat," said Chalyth wearily. "Within the clear range of historical memory there is not even the faint shadow of the knowledge to save Earth. Even if there were, there is no one alive who could exploit it—"

"That I refuse to accept," Creohan interrupted. "Does it not seem strange to you that the turning cycle we've agreed exists has stuck at one level since the time of the Mending of Men? We've had a millennium of quiescence and consolidation. It seems not to be in the nature of man to remain static for much longer than that. Indeed, unless the cycle has been broken, I would assert that somewhere on Earth people *must* be learning to build with tools and to design machines. They cannot all be obsessed with the past, or degenerate savages like the little brown men."

"How long do the Trees of History live?" Hoo said suddenly. Paro-mni, drawn out of a private train of thought, blinked at him.

"Why—we cannot say, can we? The original Umftiti trees sowed and re-sowed themselves in their grove for twenty-nine thousand years, but the process was unwitnessed by any human who bothered to keep records of it."

"Let us nonetheless return to the Umftiti period," said Hoo.

"Why? What purpose would that serve?"

"At some time in that age, may not a man have gone to a Tree and looked into a past cluttered by thirty thousand years' fewer memories?" proposed Hoo significantly, and as the words sank in the others began to laugh like condemned men reprieved from sentence in the nick of time.

XXI

INDEED THERE HAD been such a man. His name they could not pronounce—it consisted largely of a tongue-click and a grimace—and his way of life and his manner of speaking were alike strange. He had been the priest of a cult whose deity was a long-vanished animal; he wore the beast's flayed skin and his hair was plastered to his skull with clay. But he had believed in the truth of what the Trees could show him at a time when most held that the memories were visions conjured up by evil spirits, and he had stretched the past to its uttermost limit.

And he had watched the Cursiles, and the Lomril, and the Slarf, but those were the very least of what he had witnessed. The Slarf, latest of all human cultures to attempt the stars, had had success as they counted success, but their object had merely been to satisfy themselves that the stars were indeed suns like Earth's sun, as then-ancient tradition declared, and following the single voyage which cost one man a lifetime and his sanity to confirm the fact, they turned their attention elsewhere.

That, though, was in a strange, strange epoch, when it was not only such fragments of scientific dogma as the statement that the stars are suns which were being passed on as a kind of folklore, but also incredibly elaborate techniques. An apprentice in a village smithy might not know the map-shape of his own country, but in a single day he could smelt, cast and finish the metal for a power-tube sufficient to heat and light a large family house. The poorest of the poor slept in unparalleled comfort on the meniscal interface between two volumes of air, warm and dry though bitter rain might be hammering his room and freezing as it dripped off the eaves. A youth separated from his beloved would leave her for memento a walking talking doll that uttered tender words in his own recorded voice.

Glimpses of these and other wonders drove the searchers frantically further and further back, aching to know what unique culture had advanced so far that it left these miracles behind as mere débris. Since the heritage had disappeared well before the advent of the Muve, it was clear that in the time of the Cursiles only a fraction of the original mass of knowledge could have survived; then, it was taken for granted that the people of quite a small town should be able to build space-boats and send to the moon for their requirements of ore.

Yet, as they delved ever deeper, they encountered no point of origin for any of these marvels—only a series of seven successive cultures in which the shape of and means to drive a vessel to fly space were public knowledge, and very many people freely put it to use. Almost, they agreed, it was as Hoo had suggested: a breed of men once seemed to have existed who were fascinated by the vast trackless void beyond their shield of air, and gladly accepted its challenges. What had happened to wipe away this attitude? Was it merely that spaceflight became familiar, developed into a routine, and ceased to excite the imagination? That seemed incredible. The galaxy was far too big, and there was no lack of variety in the assorted reasons these seven cultures found to explore the tiny local section which was accessible to them.

Once more the visions began to grow foggy. Memories of the Tree's memory were in any case distorted by the lack of understanding their proxy of the Umftiti age brought to his studies, and it was only a matter of a month or two before they were again at the impasse they had reached earlier.

Yet they did not immediately resign themselves to failure. For there was one tantalising hint they had chanced across to suggest who had left this fantastic legacy of skills for their successors to mine, and where they had originally flourished. There was a mountain, a huge and inaccessible mountain, around which legends clustered thick as ripe fruit on a tree. A folk-tale had lasted through culture after spaceflying culture which declared that any successful assault on the stars must start from this alone of all places on the planet. So firm was the grip of this belief on the minds of later ages that time and again starships which had almost achieved success crashed to ruin on the peaks of the surrounding range. Gigantic efforts were directed to levelling the mountains, without harming *the* mountain; then the altered disposition of weight on the Earth's crust caused an upsurge of magma and the outbreak of several volcanoes, and by the era of the Slarf the tradition had been finally forgotten.

Forgotten, that is, until this man of the Umftiti decided to exile himself from his people and trek far to the west in order to find that mountain; over him too, despite his superstitions and total ignorance of machines more complex than the lever and the wheel, the ancient legends exerted an irresistible attraction. Presumably the journey had cost him his life far from human society, for hunt as they might they found no clue to his fate.

Without their ever discussing it between themselves, the same intention arose spontaneously in the minds of the five searchers, and on the evening when it was first referred to directly at their regular nightly discussion they all seemed half-afraid lest none of the others should have reached a similar conclusion.

The discovery that they shared the reaction provoked relief which almost tangibly filled the room.

"It makes good sense," said Paro-mni. "It's unlikely that there is anywhere in the world where the methods of exploring the past by means of a Tree of History have been more thoroughly developed than here. Centuries of meticulous study must surely have refined the technique to its ultimate, and if we here reach a point where no further clear information can be garnered, so too will anyone else. We must try an alternative approach. Agreed?"

"Agreed," said Creohan, "though I have no very high hopes of a visit to that mountain yielding a solution to the problem. Clutching at shadows, however, is an occupation that is fruitless by definition."

"Tomorrow, then, we will tell my grandfather of our proposed departure," Kiong-la said. "And I don't imagine he will be sorry to see us go."

"None of your people will," said Hoo. "They want nothing so much as to forget the doom hanging over Earth, and so long as we are here they are constantly reminded."

Accordingly, the following day, they waited upon Kiong-binu, attended as usual by Neng-idu and Liang-liang. In part, Kiong-la had been right. The old man did not appear sorry at the prospect of losing his long-time foreign guests. On learning that his granddaughter planned to accompany them, however, he was dismayed. In the months they had spent here, the travellers had acquired fair facility in the native tongue, and they did not need interpreters to translate the exchange between these two.

"Is your mind made up, grandchild?" Kiong-binu cried.

"It is," she replied firmly.

"But what is the purpose of undertaking this journey?" the old man pressed her. "Do you hope perhaps that on the way you will chance across a machine-building people who, in two centuries, can seek out and apply a means of turning aside a star?"

"Certainly we shall not find such people if we remain here," Kiong-la said tartly.

"Equally you may not do so on this projected trip! And if you don't—even if you win to your alluring mountain—what will you do then? Will you sacrifice the rest of your days in combing the continents for people who may well not exist anywhere?"

"If there is no one bold enough to attempt the apparently impossible, then we must resign ourselves to the fate of Earth."

"Apparently impossible? During your search winter has come and gone; after all these months have you still not located the information you were hunting for?"

"Alas, no," Kiong-la admitted, and Neng-idu gave a scornful chuckle.

"I knew from the first their quest would be a vain one. What good will it do them to find their imagined machine-making people, when in all past time the necessary techniques have never existed?"

"Perhaps this thing has never happened before," Creohan snapped, nettled.

"Neng-idu doesn't believe in things happening for the first time," Paro-mni said. "Never having had an original thought in his life! But in any case, one cannot say that the knowledge has *never* existed. It may well have done, but we can't get at it, for exactly the same reason as you, Neng-idu, are wrong in your claims about our people's project. It is absolutely impossible to analyse and document the whole of human history, and your beloved enterprise will never be completed whether or not Earth is burned to a cinder by the oncoming star."

Choking with sudden rage, Neng-idu forced himself to his feet. "How dare you scoff at the task for which your ancestors lived and died? How dare you mock us who are following in their footsteps dutifully, as they'd have wished? You—you—!"

Words failed him, and without warning he hurled himself at Paro-mni, seizing the younger man's throat in both his pudgy hands and rolling him backwards off his stool with the violence of the impact. Kiong-binu uttered a reedy cry of alarm, and the others jumped to Paro-mni's rescue, but it was Hoo that mastered Neng-idu, drawing on his old ability to wrestle with rogue meat-creatures. Almost faster than the eye could follow, he had pinioned the big man's arms, hauled him to his feet and clamped steely fingers over his mouth and nose.

Neng-idu's eyes grew round with terror and he frantically struggled to free himself. Lack of breath weakened him in moments, and when his face was purpling Hoo whispered, "If you want to go on breathing, behave yourself! I'll let you draw a little air—now, so— but if you try the same again or even so much as speak, I'll close your airways for good!"

Kiong-binu gazed at his trusted aide, overcome with

such horror that it was a long while before he could find his voice.

"Why should he have done that?" he demanded at length.

"Because he could not bear to be told the truth," Paro-mni said, rubbing his throat where the marks of Neng-idu's fingers could clearly be seen. He added a word of reassurance to Kiong-la, who was anxious to know if he was all right, and continued.

"I'm afraid I was speaking the truth," he said. "There is a barrier beyond which our Trees give us no power to explore. It lies five times as far into the past as the present range of your detailed investigations, but we are convinced you will eventually encounter it, as we did. It's as though there is a limit to human variability, and once there are sufficient similar cultures between now and the extremely distant ones confusing overtones from later periods interfere with one's studies. That's what has baffled us, and I don't think you could accuse us of lacking either persistence or intelligence."

There was a long silence. During it, Neng-idu tried to speak, and was instantly frustrated by the renewed pressure of Hoo's fingers on his face. Fuming, he abandoned the idea.

At last Kiong-binu, his expression resigned, addressed Kiong-la again.

"Go then with my good wishes, grandchild. The truth must be faced wherever it is found, and I accept that what Paro-mni has told us is the truth. Moreover, in a sense you have done us more service than merely showing us a new fact. I had it in mind to nominate Neng-idu as my successor, thinking his devotion to the cause of our people was also a devotion to the pursuit of truth. I have seen that I was wrong. Let him go, friend Hoo. Be assured he will never gain my ear from this day forward."

Hoo complied, and looking as though he was about to burst out crying Neng-idu hastened from the room.

Once more Kiong-binu paused, as though weighing his next words.

"It has come to my notice," he said finally, "that you have occasionally expressed contempt for our people." He was looking now at the travellers: Hoo, Chalyth and Creohan. "I can well see why. There is a spirit in you not to be found in many of us; I almost marvel that it exists in Kiong-la and Paro-mni. It is barely believable, but it is possible, that you will be the instrument of saving us from our own blindness. Forgive us for making your task more difficult than it need have been. Ask whatever you wish for your journey, and I shall see that it is provided.

"I wish you well from the bottom of my old and foolish heart . . ."

XXII

DESPITE THE CONTEMPT of the students and leaders
for anyone who deigned to soil his hands by working
with matter and machines, the community they were
leaving included not a few competent artisans, and in
accordance with Kiong-binu's promise the party were
well equipped and provisioned for the next stage of
their journey.

Their way lay due west, over territory which they
now knew almost as well as if they had travelled it
already, for many of Earth's lost civilisations had flow-
ered and decayed in this region without significantly
altering the face of the land. The plains and mountains
they must traverse were patient; they might slumber
through a million years, let alone mankind's puny hundred thousand of recorded history, without stirring,
while the imperceptible drift of the dust and the gentle
dissolution of leaves into mould blotted out the traces
of man and prepared yet another blank surface on the
world-wide palimpsest.

The relentlessness of the process depressed Creohan.
He could vividly foresee a time when—even if their

foolhardy quest was rewarded—men would once again forget there had ever been a threatening star to turn aside. The hugeness of natural events made man's bravest undertakings seem petty, especially when he was tired at the end of a day's walking. They were advancing into spring, having passed the winter among Kiong-binu's people, and he sought what consolation he could gain from the reflection that some of the brilliant polychrome flowers now burgeoning about them might testify to the clever intervention of men who had loved beauty. But that was of little help. Granted the work of those cultures which modified living things lasted for a while, it still might be wiped out by frost, or disease, or the absent twitches the land occasionally gave, like a sleeping giant disturbed by a fly. At every step he seemed to plant his feet among the broken shards of his ancestors' dreams, and tangible evidence to support that feeling abounded: a knoll punctuating a plain, which poked up the stub of a wall like a rotten tooth to show that it had once been a city; oddments of plastic and hollow dented metal balls cast up on the banks of rivers swollen to near-flood by the thawing of the inland snows; a certain place they came to where the sandy ground had been struck to a sort of thick glass, too slippery to walk on, in the shape of a regular pentagon—for what purpose, none of them could guess.

Even that, however, was not likely to remain for long. The cycle of heat and cold had cracked it from edge to edge, and the mycelia of a fungus had already reached clear down to the underlying soil, sucking up nourishment to grow its little glaucous knobs.

When he broached his gloomy thoughts to Chalyth, though, she answered him cheerfully.

"Creohan, it's far too soon to be so pessimistic! Maybe when you're old and stiff and bleary-eyed—not yet!

It appears that we're embarked on an enterprise without precedent; therefore the capacity for new invention has not wholly deserted our race. And who knows to what new heights it may rise when the disaster has been averted?"

Seeing that he was not much comforted, she added, "Anyway, we're making splendid progress now."

That, at least, was true. Creohan often wished he and Chalyth could have been as well prepared for the first stage of their trip as they were for this one. Not only had Kiong-binu's best craftsmen fitted them out with light tents, folding beds and the means of cooking a daily meal—something, he was sure, Madal would have delighted in—but also they could make camp for the night and say with confidence, "Tomorrow we shall go on an hour's march and come to a shallow ravine, which should by now be weathered so that we can cross it"; or "From here we cannot go straight, as the land was becoming desert three thousand years ago and is probably still barren and rocky"; or "Those trees yonder never grow far from water, so they must mark the line of the river we're looking for."

There was little incident to mar the trip, moreover. Twice or three times in the past which they had explored, hungry wild animals and wilder men had infested this area, but the beasts had long ago given up the unequal struggle after men—repeatedly—descended to the beasts' level and beat them at their own ferocious game.

Still, certain animals survived, descendants presumably of those which offered no rivalry to man. Some were long-eared, gentle, shy, and dodged away among the scrub if anyone came too close; others were gaunt, with thin limbs on which they bounced agilely along in herds too numerous for them to care about the presence of human beings; also there were plump, amiable creatures with fat tails dragging behind them and blunt snouts with which they rooted in the soil for succulent tubers.

From these creatures they learned what roots, shoots and leaves made good eating, and one fubsy monster as high at the shoulder as Creohan's waist—too fat and lazy to enjoy finding his own food—learned something in return: that humans did not eat their grubbed-up roots directly, but left them in heaps to await cooking: a labour-saving device with only one drawback, that what sufficed for all five of them was a mere snack for him.

For a while they tolerated his lumbering attendance on them, thinking they might use him as a guide to the best tuber-clumps, but in a few days it became clear that he expected them to guide him, not the other way about, and at last they had to drive him off with a firebrand. His grunts and squeals of complaint could be heard for hours thereafter, as he ponderously made his way back to his home territory.

The sight of so much meat made Hoo briefly wistful, but it was not the custom of Kiong-la and Paro-mni's people to kill land-animals, although they fished for cold-blooded creatures. It was a distinction he found tenuous, as did Chalyth and Creohan, but in view of the great assistance their new companions had rendered they abode by it.

In view of the continuing abundance of animals, it was a mystery what could have become of the folk who formerly inhabited this land. They found no trace of recent human passage, only relics of long-vanished peoples. Nonetheless, they were not downcast. A calm certainty filled them—even, eventually, Creohan, who had begun the trip in such a pessimistic state of mind—

and uncomplaining they put miles behind them between every sunup and sundown.

It did sometimes puzzle Creohan that they should be so pleased to undertake a punishing journey with no clearer notion of what lay at the end of the trail than that tantalising tale of a mountain which always endowed a starward venture with success. Yet action of itself seemed superior to waiting and wringing one's hands. That was enough justification for the nonce. Later, perhaps, some better reason might appear.

Meanwhile . . .

A hundred days brought them more than halfway to their goal. They were now traversing an especially rich region, whose vegetation was luxuriant but whose nights were bitterly cold even at the height of summer. And here, for the first time, they ran into something that had changed completely since the era from which they drew their knowledge of the area.

Across their path from horizon to horizon marched a forest of dark green trees, their trunks interlaced with creepers and underbrush into one vast dismaying barrier.

At first they were prepared to enter it anyway and try to strike directly across. A few hundred paces from the edge, however, they realised that the treetops completely hid them from sight of the sun, let alone the stars by which Creohan nightly had to plot their next day's course. Withdrawing, they made their way to the top of the highest hill in the vicinity, to see whether there was any sign of a break in that great green wall. There was none. So straight that it looked artificial, though the likelier explanation was that it followed the line of some geological discontinuity—perhaps the boundary of an area rich in a necessary trace-element— the edge of the forest cut them off from their destination.

The sun was past the zenith already. It seemed best to remain where they were until the morning. While the light endured they conducted short forays into the forest and satisfied themselves that it was indeed impassable, so tomorrow they must turn north or south, whichever they agreed upon. There was much argument over that, Hoo and Creohan maintaining that north was better, for the colder climate might inhibit the forest's luxuriance, whereas the southerly warmth would encourage it, Paro-mni and Kiong-la stressing the risk of being overtaken by winter if they had to make too long a detour and opting for the snow-free south. Chalyth offered no opinion of her own, but listened carefully to both points of view and admitted that both were impressive.

At last they wearied of the fruitless discussion and lay down to sleep, close around their fire for the sake of its barely perceptible warmth. Their tents and other belongings were proofed against the risk of burning, so there could be no danger from flying sparks. And for a long while they had traversed country devoid of menace, where even beasts larger than men took fright and hid when strangers appeared.

Despite knowing all this, Creohan found himself denied sleep by an irrational unease. In order not to disturb his companions by the noise of tossing and turning, he forced himself to lie still, but that aggravated his problem. At last, hoping to calm his mind by looking at the nighttime forest—the presumable source of his unaccountable alarm—and convincing himself it was quiet, he drew on his clothes and stole out of the tent.

He put a few more dry branches, gathered from the edge of the forest, on the fire, and they crackled up as he walked away from the flame-light, shielding his eyes to enhance his vision. The sky was wholly cloudless, and the terrible star burned blue-bright among its harmless fellows.

Over and over his mind revolved the problem which had so concerned them earlier: northward tomorrow, or southward? He struck a bargain with himself, realising it was superstition but lacking any alternative. In accordance with—

"Creohan!" A soft whisper startled him. "Is something wrong?"

"No worse than sleeplessness," he replied equally softly. "Go back to bed. I'll come in a little while— No, stay a moment. Tell me if you think it's foolish for me to divine the proper route for tomorrow by watching for a meteor, and falling in with Kiong-la and Paro-mni if its trail points to the south."

Chalyth chuckled. "I can think of worse solutions to release one from an impasse! What made you hit on this?"

"Your own words, a small eternity ago, about Earth being on our side because our cause is good."

"I still hold that view," Chalyth murmured. "Despite that obscene mass of trees blocking our route. Well, then, I'll watch with you. We'll stand back to back, and on whichever side a meteor first appears we'll fix our decision."

Smiling at her readiness to fall in with his silly notion, Creohan embraced her lightly and turned into the position she had proposed. Her head tilted back to rest on the base of his nape.

"Shall we have long to wait?" she queried. "It's not too warm away from the fire."

"A short while only," he assured her. "Near space is dense with the fragments left by the destruction of the moon, as I remember telling you the night of our first meeting."

"How far away that beach seems now!" she sighed. "And how much closer are we to—? Ah, there's one!"

In the same instant Creohan had exclaimed, "There!"

And fell silent, wondering. Overhead, almost directly at the zenith, not one but a whole cluster of meteors had flashed into sight, five, ten, fifty, in an uncountable stream, and every last one of them pointed neither north, nor south, but due west, directly across the looming dark mystery of the forest.

XXIII

A HISSING NOISE. Creohan awoke with a start from the shallow slumber into which he had finally managed to escape through sheer exhaustion, not because that curious and absurd meteor-omen had eased his mind.

The noise continued. A whiff of smoke blew to his nostrils, and on the instant he placed the identity of the sound: a fire being put out with water. Yet there was no rain—the drum-tight tent would have resonated to its beating.

Tent?

With a stunning shock he realised that there was no tent between him and the sky. It had whisked aside, flip, like a conjurer's trick. Silent dark shapes had invaded their campsite, the dim starglow revealing little more than that they were hunched, gangling, hairy—grotesque parodies of men, with arms so long they needed barely to lean forward to set the backs of their knuckles on the ground. That much he garnered from the last dying flicker of the fire, into which three of the creatures were urinating to extinguish it.

He yelled at the top of his voice and tried to jump

up. Instantly a tangle of netting fell over his head, dropped to his waist, and yanked so hard that he rolled off his bed and sprawled painfully on the ground. Before he could recover, the same treatment had been accorded to all his companions, and within the space of a few heartbeats they were trussed helplessly.

Dazed, the travellers stared at the—beasts? No, one had to say *men,* Creohan told himself—the men, then, who had taken them captivé. Their humanity was attested by their skills; of all the creatures that a hundred thousand years had seen on the land surface of this planet, only men had the ability to fashion creepers into nets, wore clothing, carried weapons and took prisoners. Not that either the clothing or the weapons appeared elaborate. As he gradually brought the tumult in his mind under control, he was able to discern that what they wore was limited to corselets and leggings of plaited leaves, giving the impression of scales, and they bore only spears. But those had cruelly barbed heads, and the presentation of one close to his throat was enough to convince him of the futility of resistance.

"Creohan!" Chalyth called, her voice muffled by the chance which had wrapped a tress of her thick hair over her face when the net fell over her head. "Creohan, I can't see! What's happened?"

"There are—twelve or fifteen people," Creohan mumbled, eyes almost crossing as he strove to watch the menacing spear-tip. "Paro-mni, you know some of the languages of this region, don't you? Try talking to them!"

Paro-mni obeyed, his voice shaking with ill-mastered terror, but their captors took absolutely no notice whatever. While one guarded each of the travellers with his spear and another held the end of the encumbering nets, the three who remained unassigned—including the tallest, whom Creohan assumed to be a leader—examined the campsite with every appearance of curiosity, turning over the tents whose guy-ropes they had slashed, lifting and snuffling at the portable beds, rummaging through their various sacks and satchels. But there was virtually no sound except for Paro-mni's desperate utterance of fragmentary greetings in a dozen languages.

"You might as well stop," Kiong-la said in a weary voice. "I don't think they can hear you. Look—they don't seem to have any ears, do they?"

Amazed, Creohan realised that she was right. At first the shaggy growth of hair on their heads had disguised the fact from him, but as he became calmer and better able to study them he picked out more details, and there certainly was a complete absence of ears on those slope-browed heads. As if to compensate, the eyes were huge, showing a full circle of white around dark centres which could well have been all pupil by the degree to which the deepest shadow failed to hamper the precision of their movements.

Paro-mni broke off. He said, "What in the world have we stumbled across now?"

"Enough cultures in the past have tampered with human heredity," Creohan muttered. "Perhaps these are descendants of a halfway successful experiment."

"But where can they have sprung from?" Chalyth cried.

It was Hoo that answered. "I know a bit about evolutionary adaptation. It sort of gets bred into you in my family . . . Out of that damnable forest is my guess. Arms like that would be kind of useful for getting around in the tops of trees."

"Well, it looks as though we're about to find out," Kiong-la said with ghastly gallows-humour.

Finished with his inspection, the one whom Creohan mentally identified as the leader made a quick gesture that concluded with a jab of his forefinger towards the forest, as Hoo had predicted, and at once the travellers were swept up in their nets, their feet cunningly tangled in the meshes. Spears were thrust through to form carrying-poles, and the band of night-marauders set off down the hill at an easy lope, the bearers frequently using their free arms as a kind of third leg over the rougher bits.

"It looks as though your omen has come true, Creohan!" Chalyth called.

"What omen?" Hoo snapped.

"I was trying to resolve the disagreement about which direction to take around the forest by waiting for a meteor to point its trail north or south," Creohan explained. "And not one but dozens of the things appeared, all pointing straight *at* the forest."

"Ridiculous!" Paro-mni said in a strange high voice. "The rankest superstition!"

"Superstition or not," Kiong-la countered, "the forest is where we're bound for."

Incontestably the forest was home to these people. The moment the black-dark trees closed in around them they seemed to relax, forgetting the caution that had made them so silent while they were on open ground. Still they did not actually speak, but they cheerfully brushed aside branches with whip-like snapping sounds, made leaves rustle and disturbed other forest-dwellers from their sleep. There were chattering beast-calls, a high shrill yammer, a basso-profundo groan.

So absolutely assured were the bearers now they were back where they belonged that Creohan did not realise when they left ground-level; he only worked out afterwards that he had been carried up a kind of sloping pathway, its gradient too gentle to slow the party down, along branch after branch and from tree to tree. At the time all he knew was that he was abruptly hoisted vertically into nowhere, swung to one side, and un-ceremoniously dumped along with his companions on to a level platform about twelve paces square, and the stars were once more overhead. Below treetop height the forest was as murky as an underground tunnel.

He rolled over and sat up just in time to see the last bearer make a fantastic leap across a pit of utter black-ness to the crown of a distant tree, seize a high bough, and drop with its yielding to another one out of sight.

They were alone, free to sort their limbs out from the nets and take stock of their situation. He was first to release himself and went to assist Chalyth, who as-sured him she was unhurt bar some abrasions which the nets had inflicted on her tender skin.

Paro-mni had suffered a sprained wrist, but other-wise they were all unscathed. Cautiously, not knowing what they might be standing on, they rose to their feet.

"What is this—this platform thing?" Kiong-la de-manded. "It's springy, and it doesn't feel very safe."

Creohan bent and explored it with his fingers. "It's a mat of interlaced branches," he reported. "It seems to hold our weight well enough, but perhaps we should stay in the middle."

"Right," Chalyth muttered. "Just looking towards the edge makes my skin crawl. Looking *down*—ugh!"

"Yes, these trees must be all of a hundred feet tall," Creohan said. "And I guess we can rely on there not being any branches strong enough to bear us within reach—did you see the way those people jumped off here?"

"What was that?"

The cry came from Kiong-la. Something had arced out of the darkness and landed with a thud at her feet. She flinched back. Another followed, and another, five in all. Hoo gave an audible sniff.

"I think that's food!" he exclaimed. He picked up

one of the objects and examined it cautiously. "Yes, a package of some sort of greasy food, wrapped up in folded leaves!"

"That—uh . . ." Paro-mni was obviously terrified, but making valiant efforts to control himself. "That means they don't want to harm us, doesn't it?"

"Needn't!" Hoo shrugged. "They might just be fattening us up for later eating."

There was a chorused cry of objection, but that was by reflex; the possibility he had voiced was only too likely on the present evidence, for they found on unwrapping the packages of food that they contained small animal-limbs coated with a battery paste and flavoured with a very strong bitter herb. Hoo tasted his, pronounced it strange but good, and ate with a will, but none of the others could muster any appetite.

Shortly still another object hurtled between them, to bounce once on the springy platform of branches, this time from a different direction. The new delivery was the shell of a nut as big as a man's head, holed at the top and re-sealed with a wooden plug gnawed into shape—they could detect the toothmarks. It contained sweet water, and they drank with more enthusiasm than they could summon for the food.

Creohan ventured to the lip of the platform, crawling on his belly, and looked down. There was a black blank chasm below, indefinably deep. He sighed and dismissed the idea of climbing down, even if their captors relaxed their present vigilance—the arrival of the food and water clearly argued that they were being watched from the still higher trees that surrounded them.

Perhaps, though, these people were exclusively nocturnal; he guessed that from their enormous eyes and their ability to manage without any light but what the stars offered. Waiting until dawn before making any decisions seemed to be essential.

The others agreed with him, and they sat down in a ring, facing outwards, at the centre of the platform. The night air was still cold, and they shivered. Bit by bit they fell silent, even though they had now satisfied themselves that the earless men were actually deaf. There seemed nothing to say which would not add to their shared feeling of misery.

Perhaps an hour passed. The most easterly of the stars paled and vanished as the approaching sun started to colour the sky. Then there was a great rustling and creaking among the nearby trees, as though a gale was stirring them, but there was little wind, and after a moment Hoo hit on the proper explanation.

"Why, the forest's *alive* with them!"

Straining their eyes, the travellers made out that he was correct. Bowing the topmost branches dangerously, there were a hundred or more of the tree-people, making weird unison gestures with their free arms. As the sky brightened it could be seen that they were screwing up their eyes so that only a slit of pupil showed between the lids. Why should they be out of the protection of the branches' green shadow when they obviously found daylight intolerable?

A moment later, the reason became clear. Hanging on a huge frame of creeper-ropes, a monstrous man-shaped doll of branches stained with red, yellow and blue dyes was hoisted up to the level of the platform. In the head of this object glinted horrible tusks and a tongue of polished new leaves, whose symbolism was unmistakable even before a spear whistled through the air past its shoulder and drove deep into the platform the travellers stood upon.

"You were half right, Hoo," Creohan said, trying not to let his own words affect him. "They didn't bring us here to eat us. They brought us to sacrifice to that— that god, I suppose it must be."

"What's a god?" Hoo demanded. "Something like what that man of the Umftiti—?"

"Look!" Chalyth burst out. "What in the world is *that?*"

They dragged their eyes from the horrible idol and whirled to follow her shaking arm, outstretched towards the sky. Far off across the black-green sea of the forest, which extended to the skyline on every side, a vast, obscenely swollen *thing* was drifting out of darkness and towards the dawn, its belly gaudy with stripes of green and white, and things like folded claws beneath.

XXIV

THEIR ATTENTION RIVETED on the five captives and the idol, and being unable to hear the oncoming monster, or indeed any other sound, the tree-people's first inkling of the sky-borne menace was belated. Another flying spear preceded it, but either the thrower was poorly skilled or he was too excited to aim straight, for this one also struck harmlessly. It was too close for comfort, though, Hoo decided, and for want of a more sensible course of action in face of the now apparently double threat they faced, he urged them to drop down and make themselves a more difficult target. All except Creohan complied.

But he, after standing frozen for a moment, did the precise reverse, leaping up and down and waving frantically—then abruptly changing his mind and bending to scrabble loose one of the leafy branches composing the platform, which he proceeded to employ as a kind of signalling flag, wagging it rapidly back and forth.

"Creohan! It'll see you!" Chalyth shouted. "Haven't we got enough trouble here?"

182

"I want them to see me!" Creohan shouted back. "Don't you know what that is? It's an airship! It's— *Aiiiiee!*"

The branch flew from his outstretched arm and he doubled over, moaning. The latest of the spears to be hurled towards the platform had found its target, and the barbs were sunk deep in his biceps. Around them globules of blood were gathering like berries miraculously ripening.

"Look out!" Hoo rasped, and flung himself sideways to shield Chalyth with his body against the risk of another spear. But now, at long last, the tree-people had noticed the thing in the sky, and they had ceased their rhythmic gesturing to blink painfully up towards it.

Paro-mni seized the branch Creohan had let fall and in his turn waved with it. The airship seemed to continue majestically on its way—or had it altered course slightly? Was the long axis now pointed more directly towards this spot?

Whatever the case might be, there was a lull in the spear-throwing. Hoo squirmed away from Chalyth towards the first of the weapons to have landed on the platform, freed it, and thoughtfully considered the targets he was offered. The people hoisting the idol by its ropes seemed like a promising one; they were bunched together on a single strong branch, and even a poor throw might well hit one out of so many.

He rose to one knee, poised the spear, and threw. With more surprise than satisfaction he watched it thunk into the belly of the endmost man, whose entire attention was distracted by the airship. The man gaped, vomited bright blood, let go his rope and toppled into nowhere. His neighbour was so startled that he too let go his rope, and the heavy idol swayed dangerously. Hoo jumped for the other available spear and sent it after the first, in order not to waste the opportunity this moment of demoralisation offered him, by which time the rope-holders had realised who was attacking them but not what they ought to do about it. As the second spear hissed towards them they incontinently jumped for safety, and the idol went smashing and crashing towards the ground.

Hoo gave a savage grin. He knew little about the proper behaviour of gods, but it seemed unlikely that deserting his people in an hour of crisis was going to encourage his followers. The next few seconds confirmed his view, for the whole nearby area of the forest seethed like a pan of green soup approaching the boil as the panicking tree-people forgot their plan of sacrifice and made for the safety of arboreal darkness.

He turned to Creohan, who was slumped forward on his knees and moaning, the spear emerging between the fingers he had clamped around the point of entry to prevent loss of blood. Chalyth, Kiong-la and Paro-mni had all moved close to him, but seemed at a loss to offer help.

"Take off that rag you're wearing," Hoo snapped at Kiong-la. Bewildered, she touched her breast and asked a mute question with her eyes; she had on nothing but the shift she slept in.

"Quickly!" Hoo insisted, and pushed Paro-mni aside to get at Creohan. Easing away his fingers, he peered at the wound. Having thrown similar spears himself a moment ago, he was aware that the barbed heads would not come loose without much pain; however, he had had experience at home with infected cuts, and he was sure that the spear must be removed quickly and the blood allowed to leak for a while to carry off any dirt that had entered.

"Brace yourself, Creohan," he ordered, and almost without pause clamped his jaw on his friend's arm.

Skin tore, muscle tore, blood leapt up and Creohan screamed like a frightened child—but the spear-barb came away as Hoo tugged the shaft and the wound, though larger now, was probably safe.

Naked, Kiong-la silently proffered her shift. He took it and made a neat dressing by tearing it so that it formed a blood-absorbing pad and two bandages to hold it in place. He worked quickly, and it was only a minute or so before the job was done.

"There!" He clapped Creohan on his uninjured shoulder. "That's not as bad as bites I've had myself from rogue meat-creatures. You'll survive!"

He glanced up as a shadow passed over them, and froze. He had never in his life seen anything like this, and the glimpses of such things he had through the medium of the Trees of History had ill-prepared him for the reality. It seemed that the entire sky had been blotted out by the vast belly of the green and white airship, and when a voice spoke from it in a language not unlike that of Kiong-la and Paro-mni his mind at first refused to accept what he was hearing.

But it was real, and in the gondola depending from the bloated gas-bag—wicker, strung on pale yellow ropes—there were a man and a woman who were evidently skilled at their strange craft of aerial navigation, for they had used the wind alone to reach the treetop platform, then grappled their vessel to it by means of cords with hooks on the end. When they had securely anchored it, they dropped ladders and came down, looking about them cautiously first to make sure there were no more of the tree-people in spear-throwing range.

"We could not come quicker," the man said apologetically. "There is not much strength in the engine which powers our ship, and we must use the wind to supplement it. But I am glad to see you all alive."

"We turned our glasses on the forest and saw what was happening," the woman chimed in. "We realised at once that we must help, but of course we thought you were some of our own folk. The tree-people are a constant threat to us, for at certain seasons they try to kidnap offerings for that nonsensical god, and daringly remain in the sunlight while they throw spears and bleed the victims to death. For the rest of the year they are little trouble, and hide in the depths of the forest."

"Are you well enough to be carried to our town?" the man demanded of Creohan.

"Well or ill," Creohan exclaimed, "I want to go there right away! You built this airship?"

"Why, yes, of course," the woman said. "Or rather not we ourselves, but our friends. It is the latest invention of my husband Roff."

"But without my wife's imagination it would not have been possible," the man said. "She is called Zayla. And you? I judge you will have strange names, since you must come from beyond the forest to the east, and that's country we have never yet explored, nor learned its various tongues."

"We are not all from the same place," Creohan said, rising awkwardly with Chalyth's help, then cradling his hurt arm in his sound one. He ran through their names, and continued. "But can you lift us all in that ship? If it's designed to carry only two . . . And to go and return might be dangerous, if the tree-people gather fresh heart and puncture its gas-bags with spears. Especially if they think to attack with firebrands!"

Roff's mouth fell open. He said, "You speak as though you're well acquainted with airships!"

"No, I never saw one before," Creohan muttered.

"Then how—?" Roff's voice failed him, and Zayla took up the abortive question.

"Yes! Even the people of our town, who saw it being built, don't realise unless they've been educated in the art how dangerous fire is to it, or how little so vast a bag of gas can lift!"

The travellers exchanged glances. There had been so much pride in Roff and Zayla's presentation of their latest invention, it seemed at the least very tactless to try and explain that this thing was not new, but had been achieved a good hundred separate times during man's chequered career on his planet. They were saved from having to talk further for the moment, however, because Creohan swayed and his face went milk-pale, and at once Zayla reacted.

"We must get you away at once! Yes, we can carry you all, I think—the wind will be against us on the way home, which will slow us down, but we have flat planes we can extend to increase our lift when flying to windward, and I think we shall skim the treetops with a bit to spare. Once free of the forest, who cares where we set down?"

Nimbly, she darted up the nearby ladder to the gondola and turned to help the injured Creohan aboard. A little dizzy with the continuing pain of his wound, he drew aside while she assisted Chalyth, Kiong-la and the others after him, Roff clambering up last of all. Meantime, he had the chance to take in the appearance of their rescuers, comparing them mentally with all the varieties of human beings he had seen either in real life or through the Trees of History.

If Roff and Zayla were typical, this was a well favoured people and rather handsome. Both the fliers were tall and solidly muscled, their skins of a gold-bronze shade that seemed to strike an average between the colour of the coastal people like Kiong-la and the brown of the ferocious little warriors who had carried them across the ocean. They wore tight garments, identical for both of them, consisting of tunics with capacious pockets at waist-level and snug breeches vanishing into calf-high boots. The fabric they were made of was expertly woven, as good as anything he had seen during his wanderings. Both had their long black hair tied back on their napes, Roff in a white cord, Zayla in green, and both wore silver rings on their forefingers, their only ornament.

All these superficialities, however, might have been matched from a dozen different cultures. What excited him was the fact that his bold prediction, long ago and far away, was being proved true: there were indeed, once again, people on the planet who were working with matter and designing machines. He almost shook with the impact of the realisation that they might well have reached the end of their crazy quest.

The moment Roff was in the gondola, he and Zayla set about lightening the craft to compensate for the extra passengers. They were ruthless about it; everything not indispensable went over the side, including their own garments. It seemed not to strike them as unusual that Kiong-la should be naked, nor they themselves, and Creohan nodded approval of the pragmatic attitude they displayed. They even concluded their task by cutting, instead of freeing and drawing up, the ropes by which they had anchored the airship.

Instantly it lurched upwards, rising a good hundred or more feet. Hoo gulped and clung to the gondola's side, but Chalyth reacted with delight and feasted her eyes on the sight of the treetops, her arm comfortingly around Creohan's waist. At the peak of their ascent Roff twisted open a valve, and steam from a small boiler at the rear of the gondola wheezed into the blades of a turbine. A screw at the stern revolved so swiftly that the blades vanished into a blur, and Zayla pulled levers and leaned on a tiller which caused the vessel to swing around in a wide curve and head back the way it had come.

Creohan's anticipation was almost painful now; he dared not utter a word for fear his hopes might prove unjustified. He waited in silence as the forest slipped away below, his stomach complaining at the unfamiliar bobbing motion but his mind too preoccupied to care.

Then, at last, the far edge of the forest came into view, and beyond it neatly tilled fields, roads converging on a town of brick-built houses, a stream in which a water-mill turned busily, many people guiding along humming wheeled conveyances who paused to stare up and wave at the airship.

Only then did he allow himself to recall the pain of his arm and slump thankfully forward on Chalyth's breast.

XXV

THESE WERE A sober and industrious people among whom the travellers had so unexpectedly arrived. Not given to acting on impulse, but patient, thoughtful and cautious, they made a very favourable impression on the newcomers. Taking the sudden intrusion of five complete strangers from some unknown quarter of the globe in their stride—as Zayla put it, accepting that the development of a radically new invention like the airship must entrain unpredictable consequences—they briskly welcomed their visitors, provided a skilful nurse for Creohan's wound, fed, clothed and housed them all without question.

Mindful of the violent dissension their news had provoked among the golden people of the coast, who had proved so unwilling to relinquish their millennium-long task of studying history, the travellers were relieved at this, but themselves put as many questions as they could without appearing inquisitive. They had been rescued from the forest people by an airship, only the third of its kind but already a safe, controllable vessel; they had been carried from the spot at which it landed in humming vehicles along a road paved with crushed stone bonded in a matrix of vegetable glue; they were accommodated in a house which to Creohan and Chalyth was unbelievably primitive, being laboriously assembled according to a plan from a stack of baked-clay bricks, but which was indisputably warm, strong and versatile in its adaptability to the requirements of the occupants; and they had consequently concluded all at once without consulting each other that here if anywhere was a community which in two centuries could advance to the point of meeting the celestial challenge.

Yet they were in no hurry to broach their secret. They were a third of the planet or more away from home—Creohan had lost track of their progress across the lines of longitude, lacking as he did a perfectly reliable standard of time, but it was possible to make rough estimates from the information the Trees of History had furnished them. At such a distance and given the known immensity of the range of possible human societies, they might all too easily upset their hosts by an incautious word.

How, for instance, would Roff the proud inventor react to the truth about his airship, which he judged to be among the first to sail the skies of Earth, yet which must be at least the millionth, for the Minogovaristo alone had built half that number to prepare and control their cloud-screened shadow-plays?

How would Creohan's nurse, adding not only his but his companions' pulse-rate, blood-pressure, respiratory efficiency and other bodily functions to her accumulation of records—because strangers might extend the range of known variability—react to being told that all these had been employed by the doctors of every single society the Trees of History could reveal to modern man?

And how, to voice the most crucial question of all,

had a mechanically-oriented culture arisen which was in total ignorance of all its predecessors?

That was likely to be a very delicate subject, they judged, and accordingly they approached it by a round-about route.

First, they willingly yielded to the touching pride of Roff and Zayla, who had made themselves personally responsible for the wellbeing of the people they had rescued from the untender mercies of the forest folk, and cheerfully undertook a guided tour of the community. Each of them encountered something of his own speciality among their hosts, or at least something of a matter which during their many months of delving into the past had particularly attracted their interest. Creohan, his wound healing well because Hoo had so promptly acted to save it from the risk of infection and able to accompany his friends sometimes on foot, sometimes in a wheeled chair for the sake of weakness due to the blood-loss he had suffered, noticed this clearly and learned things about Paro-mni, Kiong-la and even Hoo which all those long days of travelling together had not previously shown him.

"This is our friend Schrap," Roff and Zayla said, introducing a man with a thick dark beard who presided over several apprentices of both sexes in a vaulted room which stank of sulphur. "We are shut off—by land, at least—from the territories adjacent to our own: the forest, as you know, bars us from the east, because the tree-people snare intruders and sacrifice them at dawn to that imagined god who's supposed to save them from the menace of the sun's naked rays; the north is icy and the snow never melts, the south's closed off by a waterless desert, while the west boasts a range of shivering mountains, from which liquid rock runs red."

Dismayed, mindful of their intended goal—that

mountain in the west from which legend claimed ventures to the stars were invariably successful—the travellers listened anxiously.

"Schrap, therefore, hunts for methods whereby we may avoid the threats these places present to us: insulation to help a man traverse trackless snow, water-reclamation devices to take him across a desert and so forth." Thus Roff, with an all-embracing gesture. "When Zayla conceives some new refinement for one of my ships, it's to Schrap we come to see the imagination turned into reality."

There for a while they lost Paro-mni, who had been more deeply affected than was apparent at the time by the tree-people who wanted to sacrifice them, and who plied Schrap with questions about the possibility of clearing the way eastwards, towards his own home city.

Similarly, when they were taken to a room atop the highest tower in the town: "This is Lugya!"—a wrinkled elderly woman with bright eyes and an amused expression—"pivot of our community, responsible for water, fuel, building supplies, food, everything we need to conduct our lives as we desire."

There they temporarily mislaid Kiong-la, whose ambition had always been—or so Creohan guessed—to exert influence on the lives of human beings, by facilitating their mere physical requirements.

It was not something one could indulge in a place like her home city, where purely material questions were judged beneath the dignity of the scholars who explored the past.

There were artists also: a boy barely past adolescence occupied Chalyth for hours, explaining why he had shaped his flutes, harps, drums and bells just *so,* and Creohan thought of Madal and wondered how much Chalyth might have envied her secure in her beautiful house draped with yellow flowers, making

her day-long music, at the instant when her life changed
utterly and she was persuaded to set forth across the
trackless plain of high grass into which her lover Vence
had disappeared without trace. Not until this moment
had he recognised the magnificent love for Earth which
Chalyth's decision implied, and his heart ached from
his own inability to tell her how much he admired her
action.

And there were a handful of people here who were
studying organic matter in all its possible aspects, who
had theories about the origin of the tree-people and
were willing to talk the sun down and up again in
support of their views. Knowing that much of what
they agreed upon was inexact—for he had viewed a
multitude of biologically-expert cultures through the
Trees of History—Hoo nonetheless sat eagerly at their
feet, and sometimes offered a suggestion which Creohan
put down to his lifelong observation of the meat-creatures he had formerly herded and sent forth to their
deaths.

There was nothing here, like the daily arrival of
meat at home, or the wheeling of lights, to inform these
people of their forerunners; what Hoo had to say made
them marvel.

And for Creohan himself, too, there were new friends
to be made. Roff and Zayla presented him to a man
called Yade, who had devoted his life to the employ-
ment of a poor but diligently used refracting telescope,
the lenses of which he had ground with his own hands,
and who knew that the world was round, but had
not measured its size; who suspected that the stars were
suns, but had not determined their distance. Creohan
was impressed with the man's dedication, but there was
still a barrier between him and full confidence in Yade.

Yet it was by now certain that, assuming the people
would not refuse to relinquish their supposed priority

in all these technical matters from airships to telescopes, a community like this held the potential the travellers had been hunting for.

Nine days after their arrival, their mental anguish came to a crisis. As usual, Roff and Zayla—who were childless and could spend as long as they liked every day with the visitors—had come to share their evening meal of deep pies steaming-hot from the oven and little cakes dripping with honey. They were mannerly, and had never seemed irked by the way in which the travellers could keep secrets by talking in Chalyth and Creohan's language, which Paro-mni and Kiong-la understood adequately, rather than in the latter's tongue which the natives here could follow if it was spoken slowly enough.

Tonight, however, Roff and Zayla seemed tense, and the reason emerged when Roff spoke up suddenly with an air of not being able to contain himself any longer.

"Friends! Excuse my bluntness, but there's a problem which has been burning my mind since the first time we clapped eyes on you out in the forest, when you talked knowledgeably of airships yet maintained you'd never seen one apart from ours! We know from our friends that you've done the same to all of them in turn—dropped tantalising hints of improbable information, then closed up as though ice had formed across your mouths! The suspense has become unbearable. I must, *must* ask you outright: are you from some far-off city where all our achievements have long ago been surpassed, so that you patronise us as children playing games?"

The travellers exchanged uneasy glances. Realising that no one else was willing to respond, Creohan did so, and hoped as he spoke that he was capable of phrasing what he wanted to say without causing offence.

"No, we would never patronise you. We admire
your achievements tremendously, and all the more for
a reason which I shall try to explain in due time. First,
though, let me be as blunt as you, and inquire what you
know about the origins of your community and of those
others you have contacted, such as the forest-people."

"Little!" Zayla said crisply. "Our written records go
back only three to four centuries, though we suspect
they include scraps of information from much earlier.
As nearly as we can tell, our forefathers wandered out
of the west, having lost most of their possessions and
the majority of their original number while crossing the
volcanic range we've told you about. Encountering the
impassable forest, they settled here for lack of alterna-
tives, and since they resigned themselves to calling this
area home, we've done what we can to free ourselves
from the artificial constraints imposed on us. That's our
people's history encapsulated. Why?"

"Were the forest-people already there?" Creohan
asked.

"We believe so. Certainly it was not only the density
of the trees which impeded our ancestors' progress."

"And you know nothing of the place they came
from?"

"Almost nothing." Zayla started. "Why, do you
know something of it?"

"Probably." Creohan gave a sigh. "At least that
makes one thing clear—how your community could be
so in ignorance of the past. People who had been driven
from home for some unknown cause, then decimated
by crossing hostile terrain, might very easily forget a
high percentage of their former knowledge. Yet you
preserved one thing, and that may yet be the salva-
tion of Earth. You have a practical, determined, no-
nonsense attitude towards the facts of human existence
which as I told you we admire very greatly."

He glanced at his fellow-travellers. "Well, do I speak out?" he inquired.

There were nods: Chalyth first, then the others.

"I wish I did not have to tell you this," Creohan said sincerely, turning back to Roff and Zayla. "But you'll forgive me, I think, when I explain how much is at stake.

"Your airship, to begin with: you wanted to know how I could speak so exactly about its capabilities when I'd never before seen one. Well, it was because there have been literally millions of them in earlier ages. Similarly, I know that your friend Yade the astronomer has been chewing his nails over my accidental remarks about the stars. I know about them because I've made a lifetime study of them with instruments far superior to his. And, in particular, I know that one of them bids fair to destroy our Earth unless some means is found to prevent it."

Roff had been stranded at the moment of an earlier sentence, and now muttered, "Millions? *Millions* of airships like mine?"

But Zayla had listened to the end of Creohan's statement. She took hold of her man's hand and commanded him to pay attention, jutting forth her chin as though to defy a blow.

XXVI

WHEN CREOHAN HAD concluded his recital, Roff was almost exploding with suppressed anger. Leaping to his feet, he paced back and forth along the room, clenching and unclenching his fists.

"Time could not have played a fouler trick on us!" he burst out. "To think that everything we've ever dreamed of—Yade's telescopes, Schrap's machinery, our airships—has been done over and over again, and infinitely better! Why, we might as well let that star wipe us out! At least it would mean that no one else had to taste the bitterness of this discovery!"

"No!" exclaimed Zayla, likewise rising and catching at him with both hands. "You're wrong, Roff—you're more wrong than I ever thought you could be! Don't you see how fortunate we are?"

"Fortunate?" Roff gave a harsh laugh. "Oh yes! We have the luck of a man who slaves his entire life away to build a dam and protect his house from flood, only to find the river running dry!"

"No! Oh, Roff, won't you *listen* to me? Creohan and Chalyth and their friends have gone to great trouble to explain it all very clearly, and all you've done is seal your ears because someone ages ago did what you've done by standing on the shoulders of forgotten giants. Well, it's our turn to enjoy the same advantages!"

With an effort Roff mastered himself. He halted his pacing, let his hands fall limp to his sides, and shrugged.

"Very well. Show me how."

"It's simple!" Zayla's dark eyes were alight with excitement. "A new thing has come into the world within the past millennium, and it's not these—these Trees of History themselves, which the Umftiti people conceived thirty thousand years ago, and which were carried far enough over the face of the globe to have reached Creohan's city and there been used as a kind of psychological drug. No, it's the systematic exploitation of the information they provide, mapping it, analysing it, comparing one period with another and drawing conclusions—"

"But I understood Creohan to say that the people where Paro-mni and Kiong-la come from won't have any truck with mere material devices; they'd rather fry alive than besmirch their dignity!"

"Yes, but *we wouldn't!*" Zayla almost shouted. "And Kiong-la's grandfather promised all the help Creohan and his friends wanted!"

Her voice dropped, and a strain of tenderness coloured it.

"Beloved, you and I have lived together long enough for me to know how desperately you chafe against the narrow boundaries of our life. We're shut in here, by volcanoes, forest, desert, ice-packs. Wasn't it to mock those barriers that you thought of flying over them?"

Roff gave a reluctant nod.

"Well now! With knowledge of the successes and failures of almost a hundred thousand years to draw on, don't you think you'll live to fly not only through the local air, but clear around the world—perhaps even out into space? We're young yet, you and I, and neither of us is stupid. Nor is Schrap, nor is Yade, nor are all our friends. What's been done once can be done again."

"No, it can't," Roff snapped. "Creohan told us: there have been techniques based on resources which no longer exist. The buried forests they called 'coal', for example, and the mineral oils which used to be mined from far underground—all those were prodigally squandered and no trace of them remains."

"But the sun still shines, the wind still blows," Creohan said. "A magnet still draws iron and a current will still flow along a wire, the same gases abound in the air as when men drew on the processes which power the sun for their heat and light and transportation. The energy-flow of the universe is not something that's changed by the passage of a mere hundred millennia."

He could read in Roff's face the man's increasing desire to be convinced. At length words emerged that foreshadowed eventual agreement, and relief followed.

"But—but a star like our sun, only bluer . . . Does that not also mean hotter? I seem to remember that Yade—"

"No, in all respects very like our sun," Creohan cut in. "Bluer because of its velocity of approach, that's all."

"Even so, a sun . . ." Roff licked his lips. "How can we whose idea of a grand and memorable achievement is to float a hundred feet in the air and paddle against a light breeze set ourselves such a fantastic goal?"

"It will not be the first time that a group of inspired men have jumped from walking to spaceflight within living memory," Paro-mni said. "And those others had no stronger pole to vault by than myths, legends and dreams."

"Yet you yourselves have told us that in eighty thousand years of the past no people could be found with the ability to divert a star!"

"Of course not," Zayla said. With composure she resumed her seat, folding her hands in her lap. "That was left for us to undertake. It's the thing we can do which no one has done before."

Moments of silence leaked away while Roff stared at his wife in wonderment. "You're right," he said at last. "You're right and I was wrong. Nonetheless, all the people we shall need to carry out the task—where are they to be had? Not in Paro-mni's city, where they sit soft-handed and smile at the doom of Earth, nor in Creohan's, where they have no better use for the knowledge of history than to indulge their own private fancies, nor—"

"You'll find them," Chalyth said unexpectedly. She leaned forward from her place beside Creohan, giving his hand a squeeze. "I once said jokingly to Creohan that it was as though Earth herself was on our side because our cause is good. It's no longer a joke. How this can be, why this can be, I dare not guess, but it's the truth. Even in such a ridiculous matter as the meteors which forecast our passage over the forest we mistakenly thought would prove a barrier." She shook her head, and waves rippled down her long dark tresses. "I've thought about this, over and over again, and I've wondered whether perhaps those same subtle deformations of the spatial fabric which convey memories of past time to students exploring a Tree of History may not also contain a—an element of *will*, an active desire that Earth should be preserved. Right or wrong, we have the evidence. Yes, you will find the people whom you need."

"I wish I could share your certainty," sighed Creohan.

"Of one thing you may be certain," Roff declared, and approached him, extending his hand. "We shall do our part—I promise you that. Our citizens will decline to go down to the dark without at least having attempted something that is uniquely ours."

"Does it not make you glad for our species, Creohan?" said Hoo, days later, when they two and Chalyth stood on the balcony of Lugya's high tower watching rainclouds gather above the volcanoes to the west. Kiong-la and Paro-mni knew more about the recent history of this region than their companions, who had started their temporal investigations in the already distant age of the Lymarians; accordingly they were better able to contribute to a study of available resources, such as ore and water.

"How so?" Creohan muttered.

"Why, that there should still be people born nowadays who have the—the magnificent arrogance to defy the universe!" Hoo grinned in the depths of his beard. "I'm so grateful to you both for kicking me out of my home valley! There it was so easy to imagine that, if indeed there were any other survivors of our race, they too must be trapped as my family is in the rote rehearsal of actions made meaningless by the passage of the centuries. Yet you've brought me among people who are curious, possessed of initiative, determined, inclined to question everything that occurs around them. I've never been so happy in my life, nor dared to dream of being so."

There was a silence. Puzzled, he went on in a challenging tone, "Do you not agree? How can you not agree? Have you not fulfilled the purpose for which you set out from your own home—you and Chalyth both? Two good centuries of study and development, especially once Roff has carried out his intention of sending a monster airship-load of trained technicians to burrow through the accumulated data of the past in the Trees of History: won't that suffice? If it doesn't, will anything?"

"I don't know," Creohan sighed. "I can't feel sure of anything any more."

"Come now!" Hoo nudged Chalyth. "You, girl! Can't you make your man see some sense? I've told him over and over: he set out to bring information to someone who could make use of it and act accordingly, and he did so. He's probably been more successful in achieving his ambitions than anyone else currently alive on this worn old planet of ours."

"That's exactly where the trouble lies," Chalyth said quietly, and Creohan gave her a wan smile to show his appreciation of her insight. "It isn't good for anyone to achieve so colossal an ambition so readily."

"Readily! Don't you realise how fine a thread your lives hung by? Arrheeharr was within the ace of shooting you down because he thought you had been pilfering our meat; the little brown lord would cheerfully have beheaded you but for the intervention of your underwater friend; we found only two people in the whole of Kiong-binu's city who were willing to act on what we told them, and if we'd found none at all, which was perfectly possible, we'd have been chased away to wander at random and maybe starve far from human society; the tree-people might have speared us and bled us to death for the sake of their leaf-and-branch idol . . . ! You call that achieving your goal 'readily'? Then I'd like to know what you think of as being difficult!"

"That's not what I mean," Creohan said wearily. "Perhaps the root of the problem is in the different ways we came upon our common quest. Madal was well satisfied to discover people to whom she could give of her talents and warmth, and be sure in return that the gift was not despised. You wanted a sense of purpose relevant to today, not to a long-ago age. And so, too, do Kiong-la and Paro-mni—that's why they're driving themselves night and day to answer the ceaseless questions our new friends here keep putting to them. They're dissatisfied with knowledge for its own sake, the precise opposite of someone like Neng-idu who would have been content to compile his grand history of humanity and see it burned up the day the final page was written."

"Fair enough," Hoo agreed. "The universe was here before we were, and presumably it'll go on after we depart, but I see no reason to hasten or even tolerate our threatened demise. So how was your approach to this matter unique?"

"Because I'm not content either with the past or with the present," Creohan said. "I think I know now what persuaded me to accept Chalyth's challenge and set forth blindly over land and sea. I'm looking for something relevant to the future."

"To the future?" Hoo cried. "But you have it here! Care for the safety of Earth: isn't that—?"

"It's no use my trying to explain," Creohan interrupted. He looked desperate at the futility of trying to convey his true feelings.

"Obviously not! A hundred thousand years, nearly, of the past to study and draw upon, and—"

"*And how much of the future?*" Creohan shouted. "We've been here for a single tick of the celestial clock, that we can find out about! For two million years before we started to keep records of our acts, there were creatures on this planet who made fire, shaped tools, used grunts and gestures that foreshadowed speech! They too were men, my friend, and yet they had as little inkling of us as we have of those who will come after."

Hoo nodded. "True enough. Nonetheless, I am as I said content. There isn't going to be a future if we're blotted out. You've accomplished what you first set out to do, and I simply cannot understand your restiveness."

"We accomplished what we *first* set out to do," Chalyth granted. "But not what we *later* set out to do, after we'd learned the extent of our former ignorance through the Trees of History."

Creohan stared at her in mingled delight and astonishment, and she concluded to him alone, forgetful of Hoo.

"Was that not to head westward until we came to the mountain told of in so many legends? We have done all we can for these people by showing them the necessary task to engage their skills. Now we are free to go on to the very end."

XXVII

DROPPING INTO THE lee of a boulder for shelter from the bitter wind, Creohan thought of saying that he was very tired, but his mouth was as parched as a desert, and in any case Chalyth must be equally weary. The going had become worse, and worse, and then worse again, until for the past three days they had seen neither water nor any living thing bar a few lichens. Man had not dwelt in this region for countless centuries; it was a vast burn-scar on the face of Earth, bleak, racked with temblors and sifted over with ash, where the vain attempts of life to re-establish itself were repeatedly wiped out by rockfalls and outbursts of lava. The air stank of brimstone, and the sky was a louring yellow-grey.

Suppose, Creohan had often thought, that the mountain they sought had been eroded away, or laid low by one of the frequent earthquakes? Suppose, still more alarmingly, that it remained and would prove when they reached it to be nothing but a stark unclimbable crag? They did not even know if the man of the Umftiti had won to it a mere thirty thousand years before, and whatever it was that had made it of such vast importance must have taken place at least thrice so long ago . . .

Yet they had gone on—somehow: scrambling, crawling, plodding over ground that was sometimes level and sometimes steep, sometimes bare and rough, sometimes ankle-deep in befouling black cinders. How much further they could continue, he dared not try and guess. His eyes, red with tiredness, focused on Chalyth and informed him that privation overlaid her old beauty with a haggard, drawn ugliness. He knew he himself was skeletal and haggard, and he felt an ambition to become a corpse.

And then he realised she was smiling at him—a ghastly smile, cracking the layers of dust on her cheeks into wide ravines, but an unmistakable smile. He forced himself to imitate it, and in the same instant the landscape wavered and shook.

The rock they leaned against trembled, as though Earth had caught an ague. They clutched at one another, cowered, fearing the bombardment of pumice accompanying eruption of one of the innumerable volcanoes on every side of them, and shut their eyes against the gushing forth of red-hot flecks of dust.

There was a long roaring sound. There was a single crash, followed by a sliding and grinding noise: the dislodgment of a high rock from a precipice, and its coming to rest in a scree beneath as pebbles absorbed the shock of its landing. Then . . .

Creohan cautiously raised his head and looked. For the space of a dozen heartbeats the world seemed to waver on its axis before he realised that he was not suffering delusions.

Where, an instant before he shut his eyes, there had not been any mountain—only a desolate valley-floor of pumice and curdled lava—there *was* a mountain. Black.

Tremendous. Awe-inspiring. Its sides ran with water, its peak caught the dull sky-gleam like a jewel. It was *still growing*.

He tried to speak to Chalyth, but the real noise then began, the skull-hammering rage of every thunderstorm that ever was concentrated into this place and this time, the scouring of cliffs back into the sea by every ocean that ever was slamming every pebble that ever was against every boulder that ever was, and the mouth he opened to speak and the mouth she opened to answer alike remained open to let out the unison scream that neither of them could hear. The ground vibrated against their feet as though they stood on a monstrous miles-wide drum while the gods of all the human pantheons beat on its skin with thunderbolts for sticks. At last the first streams that had started from the ground washed round their feet, and they fell incontinently down to wallow in the warm contaminated water, weeping tears no less salt, blind terror driving them back to the wet security they had known, and all their ancestors, before they emerged to confront the challenge of the day.

Far off on the horizon, craters belched lava and spilled the hot seed for conception of future mountains.

He was alive. There was a hand linked in his. Bit by suffering bit, Creohan reassembled his identity from the fragments into which he had been shattered. He got awkwardly to his feet and helped Chalyth to stand at his side, both of them knifed to the bone as the icy wind slashed into their wet garments. But neither of them noticed. They simply stared.

After what might have been minutes, or might have been hours, Creohan said—very conscious of the lack of proper words to match this colossal, incredible achievement—"*Those* were the people we need today!

People who could make a mountain lie in wait a hundred thousand years, hiding beneath the ground! Where have they gone, Chalyth?" His voice was anguished. "Where have they gone, now that Earth faces its ultimate destruction?"

Chalyth had no answer, but tugged at his sleeve and led the way across the broken land.

As they drew closer, they detected an opening in the side of the mountain, not large—perhaps twice as tall as Creohan—and trapezoidal in shape. Limping, they crossed the rough heaps of rock scattered over the threshold, and saw it gave into a passageway whose walls were illumined by pale blue fluorescence, the colour of a summer sky. Beyond, something huge and powerful pulsed, as though they were entering the veins of a beast and listening to its heartbeat. The air was crisp with a scent of electricity.

They ventured inside, and instantly they began to learn.

It was not like a Tree of History, this mountain, for it held only one memory which was an explanation, and it was not alive—it was only a gigantic storage device for certain other patterns working in a human brain.

"If they could do this," said Chalyth as she gazed down the vastness of the corridor ahead, "they could move a star."

"*They did,*" said Creohan, who had gone a few paces further than she. "Be silent, and come with me."

He linked his arm with hers, and together they hobbled forward into knowledge of the greatest enterprise the human race had ever undertaken.

What name they called themselves, those far-off people had not troubled to record. It was enough that they were men and women of Earth. They had studied, and probed, and explored, being possessed by a great hunger to comprehend the universe.

So they covered the surface of their planet, and plunged beneath its seas, and trekked into its jungles and across its icecaps; they bored deep into the solid crust of their world, and soared high through its tenuous atmosphere.

When—or while, it was not clear—they were engaged in this, the moon tempted them, so they turned their scrutiny on that also. After the moon, the planets attracted them. They did not decorate the surface of their satellite with coloured vegetation to satisfy a transient whim; nor did they, like the Muve, arrogantly debase celestial bodies to a mere visible index of their rulers' fate. They were driven by inquisitiveness that at times approached obsession. What lay at the end of their trail of knowledge-collecting they never decided. Perhaps they had a vague idea it might bring happiness; more likely, to Creohan's way of thinking (for he felt he understood these people), they sought the simple satisfaction of having overcome their own puniness compared to the scale and majesty of the cosmos they inhabited.

Undaunted, they sought a means to defeat the course of the tides in Saturn's rings, and saw the sun as a mere speck from the wastes of frigid Pluto, and pierced the blazing gas of the solar atmosphere, and they found themselves on the shore of a gulf so vast that even a ray of light took years to creep across.

Unudaunted, they sought a means to defeat the natural laws of the universe. They tried to exceed the pace of those dawdling rays—and failed. There was no hope of ships outstripping light. Nonetheless, they were determined to visit the stars. Speedy, yet too slow, their vesels launched out through interstellar space, and some of them came back, to tell how there were other worlds, and beings who looked at Earth's sun and saw it as a faint white star.

But to visit even the closest of those worlds might take ten years.

They contrived to lengthen their lifespan artificially, and so proceeded for a while, but the universe was vast, and the galaxy was a mere unit of it, and nine hundred and ninety-nine thousand, nine hundred and ninety-nine parts in a million of it were out of reach.

At this time, therefore, some people began to say, "Enough!"

But others did not.

There was a paradox of available time. The best of their ships barely sufficed to carry men across interstellar gulfs, let alone intergalactic ones. Yet it had by then become plain that if only a method could be found, they had all the time they needed to explore the plenum; it would continue to exist for so long that it virtually equated to eternity.

And so it was agreed between the people who cried "Enough!" and those who did not that all the world should unite one last time on a single gigantic project. A ship could not carry sufficient numbers of men through the galaxy—but a planet could. Therefore by using the energies of the stars themselves, they brought another solar system closer to Earth and rendered one of its barren planets habitable, so that those who wished to undertake the most magnificent voyage of all might fly to it and settle there.

Then they set the star to swing on an orbit which would bring it back to Earth in a hundred thousand years, with its harvest of knowledge, and its people.

And that was where the instinct to explore the universe had gone. For the curious, the imaginative, the adventurous, were on that other world. Old habits died hard, and for a few thousands of years after the depar-

ture other men had half-remembered, and tried—out
of envy—to emulate that one superlative gesture. The
details grew blurred; the citizens of later cultures
scoffed at the improbability of legends about moving a
star; and at last the very legends were forgotten.

This too they had foreseen, that great people. Therefore they had concealed this mountain, proof against
the foolish battering of their descendants who believed
more from superstition than honest comprehension that
under this range of hills was buried the key to the
stars, designed to await the advent of the appointed
day. The electronic patterns circulating in its super-
cooled memory banks would go on, as near as made no
matter, for ever, in the hope that when the time came
for a return someone might chance to be nearby, might
learn of his race's ancient glory, and might be glad to
be alive.

XXVIII

"IT DREW US here," Chalyth croaked. "Creohan, did you feel that? It drew us here, all the way from home!"

They had found themselves outside the mountain again. They had walked blindly, lost in visions that surpassed their wildest dreams. Now, overcome, they clung to one another on the harsh barren ground, gulping in lungfuls of the smoke-tainted air and struggling to make sense of the data which had been crammed into their memories. The sky was nearly dark; they must have spent many hours inside.

Creohan coughed away filthy airborne dust. "Of course it did," he whispered. "It'll draw anyone and everyone who learns of the apparent doom of Earth and cares enough to act in an attempt to save it. No matter if they're in the Antipodes! Maybe this very moment valiant men are paddling the great oceans, or blistering their feet on the hardly-set lava of that volcanic range, following the lines of force which compel meteors to converge above this spot!"

He swallowed effortfully, and added, "I never before in my life decided to obey an omen. Do you realise

213

that? Never! For all I know that idea too was put into my head by—by *them,* who provided signs and portents suitable for ignorant barbarians in case that was all that were left. And compared to them, are we not barbarians? Look at us, will you? Filthy, shabby, half-starved, limping—wouldn't we be a fine pair to welcome home our cousins from the sky?"

She drew back and looked at him. After a moment her mouth quirked; his responded; in seconds they were laughing helplessly, having to hold on to one another for fear they might lose their balance among the loose-piled rocks.

"Ay-ay-*ay!*" Chalyth forced out at last, her breath wheezing with the exhaustion of insupportable mirth. "What a spectacle we make, indeed! But I don't think we'd need to feel ashamed. There is still something left here of the old grand spirit which took them to the stars. I think if there were not that mountain would have called to us in vain."

There was a span of silence. Eventually Creohan said, "I guess, then, we'd better go back."

"Must we?" Chalyth's face was grave.

"But we have great news to bring to our friends—"

"Great news?" she interrupted. "Will Roff and Zayla, Hoo and Kiong-la and Paro-mni be glad to have us return and say, 'There's no threat after all!'?"

"But there still may be," Creohan said. "In a hundred thousand years, who knows what may have happened on that other world? Might not our cousins too have undergone cycles of recurrent savagery, until they like us have forgotten the ancient truths?"

Chalyth shivered, and not from the bite of the wind. "It would be sad . . . But you're right, of course. No one must be shielded from the truth. We'll go, then."

Still, though, she lingered, gazing up at the now dark sky where only a handful of stars could be seen through the encircling fumes of the volcanic range. Abruptly she stiffened.

"Creohan!" she said in a changed voice. "Look there! A star that is moving!"

"I think all meteors are being drawn towards this place now," Creohan said.

"Oh, Creohan, I know a meteor—its quick flash, the faint luminance of its trail. But there is a moving light which does not fade!"

Creohan tilted his head and blinked upwards. It was true. Something was crossing the sky at a majestic pace that shone like a chip of sunstuff, piercing the roiling clouds of volcanic smoke, growing larger as he watched. On the instant, he knew what it must be.

"They've not forgotten," he whispered, and clutched at Chalyth's arm. "Miracle! Miracle! They've not forgotten!"

"What do you mean?" Chalyth cried.

"I mean that can only be one thing. A hundred thousand years ago such ships as that left Earth for another world. Chalyth, Chalyth, what it is to be alive today!"

"Then let's—" She stumbled over the words. "Let's not go back! Let's wait for them. They'll come here, won't they? They'll still remember where this mountain is?"

"Of course we'll wait," said Creohan. "If we'd only known, we'd have been waiting for them all our lives."

The spaceship grew larger in the sky. It was coming down.

About the Author

John Brunner was born in England in 1934 and educated at Cheltenham College. He sold his first novel in
1951 and has been publishing sf steadily since then.
His books have won him international acclaim from
both mainstream and genre audiences. His most fa-
mous novel, the classic *Stand On Zanzibar*, won the
Hugo Award for Best Novel in 1969, the British Science Fiction Award, and the Prix Apollo in France.
Mr. Brunner lives in Somerset, England.

From DEL REY, the brightest science-fiction stars in the galaxy...